Praise for *The J*

"Ducornet ... enlivens her illusory tale of imagination and allegory with delightful moments of humor and acerbic satire. ...There is much to be savored in this brilliant novel."—*Rocky Mountain News*

"[Ducornet] writes like a stunned time-traveler, testifying in breathless fragments to exotic ages that have gone or never were."—*Chicago Tribune*

"Ducornet has no time for realism, preferring instead an incredibly pungent, heady and violent brew of words ... in which each sensation seems to be multiplied threefold and each character is ten times larger than life."—*London Review of Books*

"While her ensemble of unearthly creatures leaps through rings of fire and enchantment, Ducornet's prose probes and flits with reasoned madness: comfortable, macabre, incantatory."—*Harvard Review*

"Ducornet writes prose of hothouse delicacy with the exquisite intimacy of a Faberge egg. .. The Jade Cabinet is at once philosophical, speculative, ornate, and self-indulgent."—*American Book Review*

"Feminists who narrowly define their 'isms' may find fault with Ducornet's novels, which are often bawdy and flirtatious, evocative of Lewis Carroll and Rabelais; however, those readers taking offense will be cheating themselves out of some of the most magnificent and merciful writing available today."—*Belles Lettres*

"Magic is at the heart of this novel—not only the magic that becomes Etheria's means of escape, but more deeply, the magic of the everyday miracles of language and memory."—*Columbus Dispatch*

Other Books by Rikki Ducornet

THE
JADE CABINET

———————◆———————

BY
RIKKI DUCORNET

With an afterword
by the author

Dallas, TX / Rochester, NY

DALKEY ARCHIVE PRESS
Dallas, TX / Rochester, NY

Deep Vellum | Dalkey Archive Press
3000 Commerce Street
Dallas, Texas 75226
www.dalkeyarchive.com

Some sections of this work have appeared in Exile and the Ontario Review,
to whose editors the author makes grateful acknowledgment. The author would also like to
thank Irene Gorak and the Eben Demarest Trust for their generous assistance.

Support for this publication has been provided in part by grants from the National Endow-
ment for the Arts, the Texas Commission on the Arts, the City of Dallas Office of Arts and
Culture, the Communities Foundation of Texas, and the Addy Foundation.

Paperback ISBN: 9781628975116
Ebook ISBN: 9781628975369

Library of Congress Cataloging-in-Publication Data:
Names: Ducornet, Rikki, 1943- author.
Classification:

LCC PS3554.U279 J3 1993
DDC 813/.54 92029129
LC record available at https://lccn.loc.gov/92029129

Cover design by Justin Childress
Interior design by Douglas Suttle

Printed in Canada

THE
JADE CABINET

This book is for Rosamond Wolff Purcell;
she brings grace to everything she sees.

Human voice is air sent out from the lungs, and by the windpipe conveyed through the aperture of the larynx, where the breath operates upon the membranous lips of that aperture, for as to produce distinct and audible sound in a way resembling that in which the lips of the reed of a hautboy produce musical sound when one blows into them.

—James Beattie, *Elements of Moral Science* (1790)

CHAPTER

1

Memory, wrote Mr. Beattie, *presents us with thoughts of what is past accompanied with a persuasion that they were once real.* The ambiguity so delighted my father that with my mother's permission I was named *Memory*—a curious coincidence considering this memoir which has seized the lion's part of my relic years. I write from the new century about the old, my purpose to reanimate planets that have long ceased to spin.

This memoir includes the reminiscences of Radulph Tubbs (his Egyptian journals and Oxford papers have long been in my keeping)— prideful outpourings touched, it is true, by an undeniable wistfulness and more: *remorse*, yet filled with misconceptions and misinformed by a certain callousness of heart—surely the greatest burden of his vast inheritance. I also quote tatters from my sister's own diary—so badly trampled by Tubbs as to be, for the most part, illegible.

To begin, then, my father, Angus Sphery, was a good man, this quality exasperated by a tendency to amplification, not to say inflation, and an insatiable desire for knowledge both worldly and divine. Angus Sphery was an eccentric and from the start my sister's life was ruled by eccentricity. (Our mother's notorious strangeness, so unnecessarily rendered public by gossips, was due to folly; up until the time of her fever, Margaret Sphery was strong-willed, even-tempered and balanced, if, for the love of Father, too eager to fly with his fancies and so share in his imprudence (for Father *would* become fixed upon an idea and not leave off 'til he had found the answer, or worried the thing to death).)

My mind nets this exemplary specimen: Angus Sphery believed that Adam and Eve had been created with navels, nipples and speech, and that if they had held on to their nipples and their navels, they had, at the instant of their fall, lost their ability to speak, and so, stumbling from Eden as dumb as stones, had tediously to reconstruct a language which, in fact, could only be a pale copy, a simpleton's stuttering—compared to the Divine Original which Father claimed was so powerful as to *conjure the world of things*. All of Adam and Eve's needs were seen to by this language of languages which was also a species of magic.

If Adam was hungry, let's say, all he had to do was utter 'roast quail' and *poof!* The quail, brown to a turn, succulent and steaming, appeared before him run through on a handy birch wand so that Adam might dine without burning his fingers.

'Lord, I'll have the cherry cobbler!' Adam cries next; Eve after: 'Strawberry fool!' (If only things were still so, I should command at once a nice slice of mince pie!)

In his attempt to uncover the keys to the universal language, Angus Sphery charted the flight of butterflies above fields of wheat, mapped the beetle's spots, copied down the patterns on the shells of winkles, on the hides of panthers, tigers, zebras, llamas and giraffes at the London Zoo, goats and cows of the field, cats in kitchens, dogs in alleys, turtles sleeping in gardens. He had alphabets of eyebrows, of his students' and his neighbours' facial moles; he ruined his eyes staring into the sky for he maintained that the Primal Language was spelled out phonetically by the planets. He spent many months living among the insane, ruining his ears with the hope that in their shrill ravings he might sweep up a few scattered crumbs of Original Speech.

Up until his experience in the asylum, Angus Sphery liked to speak of the clear relationship that existed all over the world between an object and its name. Everywhere from Bedrashen to Timbuktu a bowl of milk was a bowl of milk and a thumb a thumb. If the sounds of the words changed, their meanings did not. Father held to this unifying principle of human perception as a drowning man holds to a floating plank. It guided him; in the jumble of signification which is the world, *it was his only certitude*.

But his months among the mad at Bedlam upset him irretrievably. Here were people for whom a thumb might be perceived as a malignant tumor or a forest full of bears, and a bowl of milk as a malefic mirror. After this he abandoned his research for several years and only when Margaret Sphery was with child did the old fever return. The answer to his earlier quest lay there in his wife's womb: all he had to do was wait for the child to be born, to embrace it in an affectionate silence and await the day it would begin to speak and with its tongue untie the riddle that had never ceased to plague him.

Etheria, my sister, was the first born and I the second. By the time I appeared Etheria was mute and Angus Sphery had recognized his many grave mistakes, including an attempt to abandon Etheria, age four, a bonnet on her head and a basket of fruit and tea cake at her side, in a soft, sunny meadow circumvented by a thicket. There the fabric of the air was bright with butterflies, dragonflies and all manner of birds and the grass enlivened with clusters of daffodils. Father believed that the miracle might be precipitated by just such a place; in any case this was as close to Eden that he—terrified of public and private transportation—could reach on foot. As his daughter, wrapped in a blanket, napped among the flowers, Angus Sphery stole away. It is fortunate, perhaps miraculous, that my sister, who from the age of two kept her apron pockets stuffed with little stones and shells and such, and having in play dropped these onto the path through the woods, easily found her way back to Oxford. There a laundress, familiar with my father's house and recognizing her at once, swept her up and tucking her into a tub of clean linen, gave her a kiss and got her home again. There, or so the story goes, Margaret Sphery went into such a tantarum Angus vowed never to abandon his daughter again. The sound of those agitated voices had a profound effect upon my sister who, until then, had never heard a word. She held her little hands to her ears and, heaving, wept a steady flow of slow and silent tears.

Yet Angus Sphery persisted in his idea that the languages of men are but impoverished translations; that somewhere in the universe there exists a language of pure, unadulterated light in which even ugly words such as *hassock* and *antimacassar oil* 'palpitate as a medusa in the sea and scintillate as a comet in the sky' (an idea that so delighted Mr. Dodgson that he once sent Etheria and me a letter in which figures a bottle of *antimatter* oil bearing a luminous crown and pair of angelic wings. The Holy Grail stands beside it and indeed one cannot tell the one from the other).

The outcome of all this is evident: Etheria grew up speechless and yet for all that tremendously clever. Angus Sphery adored his eldest daughter and doted upon her. He quickened her mind by showing her all manner of curiosities (our father was a natural historian) and by way of gesture and expression and little drawings much like hieroglyphs, explained their nature or function so that from the start her mind was unusually sound, capable and curious. For example, just as the philosophers of Swift's *Travels* communicate by showing objects to one another, so Angus Sphery made Etheria acutely aware of the affinities between the eyes upon a moth's wing and a human eye, the woolly head of a sheep and a cauliflower, an oddly forked carrot pulled up in the garden and the human figure. As a babe she was already cognizant of the intimate kinship of all things, animate and inanimate. Etheria knew that the visible world was little more than an infinite game of castles in Spain built in the air with the same building blocks over and over again.

By the time I was born my sister was six and set in her ways. She was lively, delightful, clairvoyant in spirit and *silent*. Margaret Sphery insisted that the charm be broken; words entered, whispered at first, into the house. It was evident that if Etheria still refused to speak, she was an avid listener. But ever true to his vision of Eden, it saddened Father that I was learning what he called 'unnatural speech.'

Angus Sphery was also a great admirer of Lord Monboddo who already in the eighteenth century admitted to the fact, later demonstrated so neatly by Mr. Darwin, that the ape, and notably the orangutan, is a close relative of man.

'Man lost his tail through friction,' Monboddo said, 'and disuse.' Sam Johnson ridiculed Monboddo and for that he was entirely absent from our education, Etheria's and mine; we grew up venerating the obscure lord but knew nothing of Boswell and his Johnson.

A memory I cherish above all rest is of sitting in my father's lap, my head nestled against his chest, Etheria on the floor, her head resting on Father's knees. He tells us stories of the Nicobar Islands inhabited by a race of men with tails like cats; savages who run naked as the night and converse with one another by uttering the shrill, persistent cries of bats. When later that summer Dodgson photographed my sister and me for the first time entirely naked, we referred ever after to his rooms as the Nicobar Rooms.

As Etheria had requested to be photographed with a tail, spotted or striped, and had made a little drawing to that effect, Dodgson had procured one from a theatrical supplier's in London and a pair of ears. These she would not wear, only the tail which rode the crest of her buttocks with an unintentional coquetry so arch Dodgson informed her that she looked 'far too savage altogether,' and the photograph she hoped for was not taken. He dressed us instead as angels, wings of sequined silk attached to our naked backs, and tinsel garlands on our heads. In this picture, Etheria, seated upon a cloud, looks darkly beyond the picture frame at the cherished tail abandoned on the floor. I, age three, am biting my thumb so as not to muddle the tableau by moving. After, dressed in Dodgson's silk kimonos, we took tea. Etheria drew for him a picture of the Nicobar Islands to justify her disappointment. Ever after he called us 'the Nicobar Girls.' The mysterious odour of collodion permeates these memories.

I should add that at the age of nine Etheria was already so beautiful she caught the breath of men and women alike when they saw her in the street. Her dumbness gave her a certain poise and an uncanny quality; it sealed her off and thus made her self-contained. And because at an early age she had learned to express herself with wonderful little idiosyncratic ideograms of her own invention so clever they could be deciphered at a glance, she had a special quickness of the mind all her own.

She was from birth very blonde; her skin, too, was blonde. (Our father called her his 'golden child.') Her eyes were set wide apart; violet, they were enormous, oval. Her nose was delicately arched and her mouth a sensuous smear, like the crushed petals of some exotic flower, or a halved plum. I was like her, yet not so; my own blondeness far too fragile, tending to freckles and warts, my eyes set even further apart so that I always was a little peculiar-looking. Those who knew us both could not help but think that if the dice had been kissed before being tossed, I could have been beautiful too.

As it was, we were loving friends, accomplices, never rivals. I was her chief interpreter, which made up for other insufficiencies.

CHAPTER

2

There are those who say that the memory is like a collector's cabinet where souvenirs are tucked away as moths or tiny shells intact. But I think not. As I write this it occurs to me that for each performance of the mind our souvenirs reconstruct themselves. The memory is like an act of magic.

Angus Sphery witnessed the tornado of 1792 and the great eclipse of 1793. He recalls a time when sheep grazed the downs and deer strolled the campus. Twice he participated in the *perambulations*. Dressed in red trimmed with fur, he, the mayor and a great many others mostly in rags, traced the boundaries of Oxford on foot and in punts. He called it a 'glorious scramble.'

Father's especial passion was entomology. There are those who abhor insects but most have wings and this alone should assure our admiration. Mr. Dodgson once said that flies and mosquitoes are the materialisation of vowels and consonants uttered by fools and that this explains why there are so many of them.

In his youth Father had spent countless hours among the flowering lavender listening to the beatings of the wings of butterflies and even the faint sound of a spider's web lifted in the breeze or the voices of crickets because he believed that here were to be found the keys to the sacred syllables of that elusive language which already as an adolescent he longed to know. Once, when he unexpectedly heard the sudden, exhilarated hum of courting cicadas, he was certain he had been given a glimpse of the melodious order, the sweet tongue that permeated everything with meaning and with majesty.

Father's study was an especial place. He had a library of lepidoptera pinned in rosewood boxes that are now lost—thanks to a certain odious creature (for the moment in the wings). In early childhood I believed Father when he said that these boxed creatures were books with stories written on their very bodies. (And here I might add that other people have come to the same conclusion. For example, the magicians of ancient Persia assumed that the stripes and spots on the backs of animals were legends transcribed in symbols.)

Angus Sphery knew his daughters would not harm the precious things he loved and we so admired, and thus he allowed us to roam his rooms freely. He set aside for us a long oak table and two ornate chairs fitted with high cushions where we painted our own 'Butterfly Books.' I was five; Etheria eleven. Following Father's example, we also penned little treatises on natural history. A particularly lovely one Etheria made for Mr. Dodgson which she titled (if she still refused to speak, she was, at last, learning to write): *On Insects Eyes*. She also gave him a fashion book for fairies: their dresses, hats, parasols and theatre capes made with the wings of dragonflies. (How I wanted to own that book myself!)

I am convinced we were the only little girls in Britain to play 'Hunt the Thimble' among bottled snakes and tree frogs, and 'My Lady's Slipper' beside a fully assembled skeleton. How insipid our dolls seemed when we returned to the nursery after a joyous afternoon in Father's study, solving our favourite Red Sea puzzle beside Angus Sphery's stuffed orangutan (whose name was Dr. Johnson). (And this recalls the long hours we spent with Father at the London Zoo attempting to overhear the conversations of gorillas. The saddened creatures, far from their habitat and tribe, had nothing to say. Even now I cannot catch a whiff of keeping medium without wanting to weep with longing for our father's study—that enchanted playroom—and to tremble with an undecipherable excitement.)

Our favourite toys were the ones made us by our dearest friend Mr. Dodgson: miniature kites to fly in the kitchen above the steaming kettle, a paper bird that whistled when dropped from the laboratory windows and a lily pond of painted cardboard containing paper crabs and sirens and one magical fish: *Ask! Ask! Ask me a wish!* penned on his two sides and which we fished with wands equipped with scarlet string and bent pins. It was he who gave us the pinky orange dormouse that once caused Radulph Tubbs to sneeze so dramatically he was forced to leave the house even before he had a chance to remove his perfumed gloves. (This happened several years prior to Tubbs's courtship of my sister.)

We were fortunate children, especially for the times. We never wore shoulder yokes and the strongest medicine to pass our lips was licorice. We were raised to ridicule bustles and corsets and were the first in our circle to wear bloomers (for which we were severely ostracized by several girlfriends and their mothers). So it was all the more extraordinary that Etheria, my adored sister, who was so delicate and dreamy she appeared to levitate an inch or two above the ground (despite the fact that in her exuberance her shoes were always scuffed and her hems stained grass green—for she was forever prying into the boles of trees and anthills) should marry a man who *wouldn't* remove his frock coat even when he played croquet! A man who *would* flatten the landscape, make it *perfectly flat*, and house his workers in subterranean alveoli and build *pyramids in England*! A man in whose house embroidered bellpulls like dead boas hung from every ceiling.

During the courtship I once had occasion to see Tubbs's house, those multiple mirrors which spoke, if silently, of his vanity. . . I confronted a particularly odious soup tureen of polished pewter, salt cellars in their exaggerated magnificence struggling to outdo the chalices of popes; I saw Tubbs's brass knockers, his fenders, his idiotic samovar the size of a public fountain, his oversized pipkins.

The man kept a barrel of Stilton in the pantry. He sliced into it at odd hours, dunked the cheese in a glass of port and chewed dreamily, *surely*, wrote Etheria, *the only time he dreamed.* (He'd have, like a cow, to chew to dream.)

Poor Etheria! The stress and chagrin caused by our mother's chronic malady (itself precipitated by Tubbs somehow—but this I will divulge in due time) had ill effect upon our father's mind or he would never have consented to the marriage. I too feel responsible. Because Father was so wonderful, Etheria and I knew just what a father should be but had no notion whatsoever as to what a husband should be. Tubbs did seem very 'husbandlike' to us: his size, his substantiality, his handsome coat, profile and heavy whiskers. In person Tubbs was a splendid animal, near faultless, of large and vigorous frame and a brass stomach. In spirit he was a hotbed of unbelief.

Another thing. My sister and I rarely heeded him when he spoke. He made the air so heavy with his buzzing and his droning that I believe we were nearly always half asleep in his company. Etheria was particularly prone to revery, and Tubbs was a puissant soporific.

I vaguely recall when he first described his Oxford house to us. It seemed an exasperating maze of rooms for every conceivable activity in-cluding clothes brushing and silver polishing. There were plate sculleries, shoe rooms, lamp rooms, separate cheese, fish and meat larders, and closets which he described one by one—all forty-four of them! The house contained multiple passageways too so that neither butler nor maid need ever be seen unless rung for (those beastly bell-pulls); these passageways explain, perhaps, how Etheria was able to escape undetected.

I also noticed that Radulph had an unseemly predilection for maraschino jelly which he ate with everything from lobster salad to fowl. Etheria seemed oblivious to him most of the time, 'floating in thought' or 'swimming in dreams' as Margaret Sphery called it. I knew she hadn't been listening to Radulph whatsoever when from beneath the table she passed me a note:

I just recalled when Dodgson said that the sea makes him weep because it is never the same from one instant to the next and so is lost to him 60 times a minute!

Father, on the other hand, kept us wide awake at table. He told stories we loved to hear about the 'Great Moments in History,' the Flood, the Death of Socrates, the Beheading of Louis Seize; when he told us about the Burning of the Library at Alexandria we were scandalised, but not when he described the odd breeding habits of elephants.

Before going into Etheria's marriage to Tubbs, I wish to speak of the terrible change that took place after Mother's illness. Until then our family had lived in clarity; I should say: luminosity. Margaret Sphery was a wonderfully *curious* person. She was fascinated by our father's work and had her own collection of live insects. A giant phasmid (or stick insect) from India whose cage was over two metres tall spent long hours standing upon a perpendicular branch and staring into Mother's eyes. The proof of this complicity: whenever Mother approached the cage the insect would take to its branch and assume the pose which enabled them both to see eye to eye in comfort. Her crickets she had trained to chirk simultaneously by prodding the silent ones with a straw and rewarding the others with drops of sweet water. But her favourite insects were the tiny lacewings—so graceful and so green and which on summer nights cluttered the white counterpane in such quantities that Angus Sphery called them 'an ambulant embroidery.' These creatures were fed dew from Margaret Sphery's open palms.

'Your mother,' Angus Sphery once told his daughters, 'is a Faerie Queen.'

Needless to say, Tubbs asserted that insects were the enemies of man. As its inventor eclipsed to America with the formulae, no one may appreciate the composition of the poison which caused the deaths of several thousand 'ant-t-mite' cotton-swaddled infants in the summer of 1862. (The very summer Dodgson rowed up the Isis with our near neighbour Alice Liddell and told her, for the first time, his celebrated story. How often I've wished that Etheria and I had been of *that* historic party!)

That same year in the early autumn, Dodgson, Mother, Etheria and I all went to the Fruit Fair; Father was occupied with classes and the intensive study of domestic cats. (He came to the conclusion that if their emotions were complex and various, their vocabularies were limited to the barest essentials.)

To return to the Fair; there was something ridiculous about the oversized vegetables and Mr. Dodgson swept us up in a game of whimsy that went something like this:

Margaret Sphery: 'Good gracious! Just look at that marrow!'

Mr. Dodgson: 'He does look a self-esteeming fellow!'

Etheria: *Pretentious : and : Disagreable!*

Mr. Dodgson: '*Disagreeable!* Why—he's squashed all the others on the bench! The onions can't get a word in edgewise!'

Margaret Sphery: 'They *are* deadly still . . .'

Myself: 'He's ordered the onions admire his silly gold star in silence . . .'

Mr. Dodgson: 'Which he won slicing cucumbers!'

Etheria: *No Honour There!*

Margaret Sphery: 'Tremble for your life, Sir! The cook will be here directly!'

Mr. Dodgson: 'He'll butter you up *proper*, I fancy!'

Etheria: *There's Glory for you!*

Margaret Sphery: 'Now see what you've done! He's quite green with grief!'

Myself: 'Poor thing! He did *so* dream of being elected to Parliament.'

Dodgson: 'Yet I've told him one hundred times if I told him once: there are enough pumpkinheads as it is!'

Pumpkinhead! We delighted in such words. Threadneedle Street. Ned Nettlebed. A game called 'Hazard.' Jokes such as:

Q. What is the fastest cut of beef?

A. The brisket!

The day was a delight from start to finish. There were oyster stalls set up with scrubbed tables and benches where we were served little chipped dishes of shellfish nested prettily in seaweed. For dessert we bought ice cream from an Italian boy, slim and handsome, who wore a beautiful red and green sash and whose exotic-looking crow dressed in a ruff of turkey feathers cried: 'Ho-Hokey Pokey!' to the crowd. We gorged on fruit pies and peaches with white flesh and scarlet pits. The fresh cider was irresistible and we could not have finished the day had it not been for the 'ladies' tent' where on a circle of grass chamber pottery of all shapes and sizes had been set out helter skelter. Attendants wearing long white aprons helped the ladies hold up their voluminous skirts as eyes to Heaven and lips pursed, country wenches and bourgeoises alike pissed as sonorously as mares or, blushing, tinkled nervously. The attendants received pennies for their services and as their pockets were very full, they jangled like Gypsies whenever they moved. Etheria's pot was French and had an eye painted on the bottom. She refused to use it and was given another.

We returned home clutching sweets in screws of paper, happy but exhausted, our nostrils rimmed with dust. The following day Mr. Dodgson sent us a wonderful drawing of oysters munching hay in stalls and 'resting up,' he wrote under, 'for the race. Next year we'll stay for the race, but as it takes them a *very* long time to run (they haven't any feet you know), *this* year's race is always *next* year's race anyhow. So you see, my darlings, you haven't missed a thing.' And he included a receipt which 'has been proven to cure 'olds, weasels, hopping cough, the bumps, chicken rocks, the vague, hills and *growth*.'

CHAPTER
3

Radulph Tubbs was the grandson of a catsmeatman and a corkcutter, yet the smoke from the factories he inherited from his father—a daring, determined rascal who 'single-handed grasped his life by the bootstraps of his will'—is breathed by Englishmen and Englishwomen of all ages everywhere.

The elder Tubbs's ingenuity showed itself from the time he employed shipwrecked sailors in the spinning factory on the Pennines. Later he was to employ orphans—'all of whom attended church and were allowed to whitewash their quarters annually.' By 1815 every Englishman alive wore an article of Tubbs's cotton beneath his trousers (and the same could be said of corpses). Always ambitious, father Tubbs put his profit into powerlooms. The factories of Middlesex and Surrey are to my mind the most pretentious edifices of their kind anywhere. But these pages are not meant to be a history of Tubbs's Mills, although the thought has more than once occurred to me; instead it is the story of Radulph's passion for my sister.

Radulph first saw Etheria in our father's house. She was then a child of ten, an incorporeal favourite of Charles Dodgson, and she was wearing a simple summer frock of white linen. She had made for herself a necklace of morning glories and as Tubbs writes in his journal: 'The blossoms glowed extravagantly about the nymphet's neck.' She did not acknowledge him, but stared instead at her own white shoes stained green. Tubbs did not think of her again until summer's end when she burst in upon him and Father in Father's study as they sat together bibbing port and discussing the fanciful drawings Angus Sphery had made of airships inspired by his knowledge of flying beetles. Tubbs was exploring the possibilities of their manufacture, a project that never materialised. As Radulph describes the scene, when Etheria saw him she frowned, stilled and paled as if in that instant she had intimated all that was to pass between them. It is surely true that at this second apparition, her supranatural beauty impressed itself upon him. Thus began Tubbs's time of waiting. Always an impatient man, he animated the exasperating years to come with brittle pleasures too thin to number.

That first summer of his love Radulph Tubbs made discreet enquiries; he learned to his dismay that he was not Etheria's only admirer. It rankled him to learn that Dodgson was often invited to dine whereas he—despite the intensification of possible business relations with our father—received but port and cigar in the study. A cruel blow to Radulph's self-esteem; until then he had easily charmed his way into the drawing rooms, dining rooms and bed chambers of most anyone he chose.

Tubbs instigated his first investigation into our private lives. He learned that the 'Dodo' sent Etheria many delightful gifts, making any attentions on his own part redundant. 'Apparently Dodgson's cleverness is boundless,' he wrote; 'the games he brings the girls, all of his own invention, are stamped with a peculiar genius.' He adds, 'How am I to compete?'

When Tubbs discovered that Etheria and I had posed for Dodgson in the nude and his obsessive interest led to an insidious campaign of slander, several people broke with Dodgson. Mrs. Liddell, who until then had favoured his company, grew distant. Moreover, in later years when Radulph had married my sister, he paid enormous sums to discover the whereabouts of the precious photographs, and destroyed as many as he could. As Dodgson never kept his plates for fear they find their way into unworthy hands, these pictures, which were—I am convinced—among his best (for Etheria illumined everything she touched) are forever lost to the world. Of Dodgson, Radulph wrote:

'However, I need not have thought of him as a serious rival. He befriended little girls between two ages: infancy and puberty. When Etheria turned twelve and put forth those upbudding breasts I had been so anxiously seeking, he lost interest in her, or, perhaps, could not face the disturbance this new manifestation of her beauty caused in his own flesh, who knows?'

Balderdash! Dodgson was as invisible to Radulph and as incomprehensible as was Etheria. Or anything lucent and quick.

By the by: I feel it is fitting that I say here what an utter delight it was to run about in Dodgson's cosy rooms unfettered by buttons and braces; to try on all manner of odd tatters, to sit, enlaced by Etheria or plaiting the cloud of her hair before an imaginary seascape, whilst Dodgson told stories about the trials and tribulations of shellfish and sea turtles; how—this I remember well—an eagle enamoured of an eel sent her a new box of croquet balls which she took for a case of Moroccan oranges. The story ended tragically.

If Radulph's life bears the imprint of a chronic dishonesty, his memoir is most candid. For example, he describes an afternoon when having taken leave of our father he crossed Dodgson on the threshold; Dodgson had been asked to dine, Tubbs, as usual, had not. In his hand Dodgson carried what was undoubtedly yet another gift for the girl Tubbs adored. When Dodgson doffed his hat, a small piece of paper fluttered to the ground. Unaware of his loss, he continued on into the house. Radulph picked the paper up and put it in his pocket. Later when he read it he was enraged and perplexed: whatever was written there was written in code. (It did not, *could not*, occur to Radulph to hold the paper up to a mirror, yet surely that would have solved the puzzle!)

That night Radulph inflicted his confusion upon a woman of 'little interest' and with whom he was determined to break. 'My own brother,' Tubbs writes, 'has often condemned my fickle character and brusque manners. The woman received my rude intrusion upon her person with a certain grace; after, her desperate attempt to retrieve from my silence a particle of affection revulsed me further. What I wanted was the impalpable sprite who, if not yet put to bed, was likely in the damned stutterer's lap listening to the insipid intricacies of a fairy tale. (I myself have never been "clever.")'

When Radulph's fading mistress battled for her lost dignity, biting her lip and fighting the tears he knew would, after his departure, torture her throughout the night, he felt revulsed with himself as much as with her and wondered if wealth was not a two-edged snare, for it had brought him more costly flesh than he could chew or digest. But this dark thought precipitated a pleasanter consideration: when the time came to court Etheria openly, his money would compensate for his age. As it turned out, it was not Tubbs's money but the *jade* that settled it: just as Etheria was claimed by puberty, Radulph inherited the family fortune: the mills, the houses and a fabulous collection of jade.

'Ironically,' he writes, 'I myself had no admiration for it—incomprehensible vessels, bugs, beasts and other bric-a-brac squatting like toads in a terrarium.' But our father, Angus Sphery, had long entertained a passion for jade because it seemed to him it held an inert script, a significant quiescence that mirrored exactly Etheria's silence. Already an undergraduate he had sold most of his books to acquire a 'mutton-fat' cane pommel, and at my sister's birth had presented our mother with a pair of pale green earrings. Since that youthful extravagance and that gift, our father, a professor of reputation but meagre salary, had put all thoughts of further acquisitions aside.

Now I shall allow Radulph to speak of himself for himself (this from his Oxford journals):

'Etheria's father often said that "beauty is the vocabulary of the soul." I myself—apart from the feminine form, a fine port, certain wines, a nicely browned piece of beef and pudding—have never been "moralised" by it. I enjoy life's embellishments and am used to elegant living, and I suppose I might feel differently if Beauty were lacking from my life. For example, I should very much dislike to find myself constrained to a furnished room on fish street above the oyster stalls. Attention: I am no "rosebud," simply: I am a man of taste, yes, and of a substance cemented by *rational thinking*, not by "beautiful feelings" or idealisations, fairy castles of the mind. I, unlike some I know, believe in the so-called external world. (But tell me, is there another? If so—*show* it to me!)

'I do appreciate oratory; I like rhetoric. I am fond of a good, solid piece of architecture. I even admit to having looked upon sculpture (of the female form and horses) without dissatisfaction. I dislike painting, its tendency to hyperbole, the way it peels and darkens with age. I firmly believe that if a thing cannot be said once and for all with *clarity*, then it is best left unsaid. The world would profit if the greater part of the poets—all panting over sunrises they never once awoke in time to see—were swept under oblivion's carpet. Give me a herring for every poem that has ever been written that I may heartily sup.

'Back to sculpture. I admit to memorials—fitting extensions of architecture. Public parks would not be what they are without them. I've *done* Italy and Greece, explored, briefly, those accumulations of rubble for which those countries are notorious. I was appalled that no attempt had ever been made to clean up the mess. It is the *uselessness* of all that riddled marble, as well as its blatant untidiness, that continues to grieve me.

'Such thoughts have I, until now, kept to the privacy of my own mind, as, astonishingly, they are not popular. I'd purge the world of its shattered temples and in their place set down factories. What is more "beautiful"—in all ways—than a well-designed factory, sturdy and square, bricks sweating and chimneys erect and belching the perpetual caul of that charmed infant:

INDUSTRIALISATION?

'I was born a man of sense; a rational man. Of this I am not ashamed. Why should I be ashamed? I continue: Beauty must and will be subordinate to the demands of logic. For example, there is no reason why a bridge, water tower or cannery could not be both handsome and functional—as any pretty woman destined to give birth to a new generation of men. . . .

'I once proposed to Etheria's father* during one of our little port-bibbing talks, that he imagine a world in which Beauty was blessedly absent.

'"We'd still have *substantiality!*" I told him.

'"No doubt," he replied. "But we would not have Etheria." This, I had to admit, was true.'

---

* How rarely he mentions *me* in the diaries!

CHAPTER
4

Handsome profile and wealth aside, Radulph Tubbs was a man of no especial endowments or graces and certainly not known for generosity. However, it was a rare and seemingly spontaneous gesture of extravagance which led to his engagement to my sister.

As I have said, Tubbs's inheritance included a spectacular collection of archaic jade that caused much excitement at the High Table; indeed, for some time, Oxford gossip concerned itself with little else. Soon after the ebony cabinet and its precious contents were delivered to Tubbs's home on Bear Lane, Angus Sphery asked if he might see them. Tubbs sent a carriage off at once to fetch our father.

The cabinet was Ming and of sober elegance, and the jade of such rare perfection that as he fingered them our father trembled. Again and again he returned to a piece that Radulph disliked particularly, and although he really could not have cared less, Angus Sphery informed him the jade represented an insect, a cicada. To Radulph's distaste Father pointed out the wing covers, and turning it on its back, stroked the insect's abdomen, which was carefully crenellated.

'It is the colour of boiled spinach,' quoth Tubbs.

'Han period . . . southern China . . .,' breathed my father. 'A protective amulet . . . to be placed on the tongue of a corpse.'

'Dreadful!' Tubbs's dislike of the thing was boundless.

'An expression of faith. And hope.'

'Faith? Hope? In *what*?'

'Afterlife.' The jade glowed in Angus Sphery's hand.

Tubbs shook his head in disbelief. The idea that the pagan Chinese expected Eternal Life was ludicrous.

'Take it,' he said, pressing his hand over my father's and the object which he held so carefully. 'If it gives you pleasure.'

'O, no! I couldn't. . . .' Angus Sphery made to put the jade back on its shelf, yet still he held on to it. 'I could never accept such a gift!' Laying his spectacles aside he scrutinised the stone, then walking to the window drew aside the curtain and languorously held it to the light. 'I have no way to thank you.'

'But you do! Indeed you do!' Radulph Tubbs said mysteriously.

'You are too kind. . . .' Angus Sphery was fingering the wings, the thin, almost transparent, pink-hued ridges of their delicate striations, stroking the blacker underside. 'I can think of no way—!'

'Invite me to dinner,' Tubbs boldly ventured.

'Dinner?' Startlingly Father licked the creature's belly briefly with the tip of his tongue. 'Dinner. Curious you should ask! Only this morning I was speaking of you to my wife. I said: "It is about time we invited my friend Radulph Tubbs to dinner!"'

So began Etheria's courtship. My sister was thirteen. Tubbs brought her a present: a large volume bound in dark brown leather, published at his own expense and containing photographs of all his manufactures: spinning factories, mills, bleach and dye-works. Imposing edifices all, solid and stately, always of the same tedious brick, the 'felicitous turgescence' (Tubbs's words) of the blackened chimneys rising as 'puissant obelisks' in the air. A weighty volume, saddeningly thick. Tubbs had chosen the heaviest paper he could find and for the frontispiece had commissioned a portrait of his own father executed in drypoint—a stern face made to radiate in the sky, an industrial age *Roi Soleil* hovering over the historic Pennine Chain installations, *now in decrepitude,* he informed us, but soon to be refurbished. In pride he pulled on his moustache.

'Here in one modest volume,' he pontificated to Etheria who was close to tears, 'are contained the three-tiered Lancashire operatives, so like fairy castles; the marvelous oil furnaces of Surrey (the corporate headquarters) and the famous "black hole" at Westminster (what castle

worthy of the name does not brag a prison?).' Over a 'beautiful' piece
of beef, Tubbs informed us of his master plan: to one day construct
three pyramids of the same brown brick upon a flattened landscape, a
leveled area within walking distance of Canterbury and 'dwarfing the
cathedral itself.'

'Pyramids?' The madman's future mother-in-law frowned. 'What
on earth *for*?' Margaret Sphery, until then silent, sucking her distaste
like a sour candy, was out of patience.

'You will be impressed,' Tubbs told her, 'when I say that two pyramids shall be symbolic silos—because hermetically sealed—containing
cotton (and the best my Egyptian holdings have to offer) and the third
of *solid brick*—all symbols of England's economic stability. There are
some of us, Madam,' Tubbs lowered his voice dramatically, 'whose plan
it is for England to become *the World's Own Workshop!*'

'You employ orphans . . . the children of destitute families.' It was
less a question than a statement of fact, and thrust upon Tubbs with
ill-concealed anger.

'And so keep them from mischief, from leaching upon society as
Miss Louisa Twining would have them do.'

As Tubbs and Margaret Sphery sparred, what was Angus Sphery
thinking? He was not following the conversation, his expression was
dazed, the gravy had congealed untasted on his plate, he was fingering
something, fingering the piece of jade that he carried with him everywhere
in a little silk pouch in his pocket.

'Miss Twining is a friend of mine.' Our mother spoke again.

'Well then! Well then, you may tell her,' said Tubbs as if to a petu-
lant child, 'that the idea of sending beggars to school is preposterous!
They must needs be *constantly* threatened, coaxed and thrashed if they
are to complete their tasks. Imagine asking such animals to learn the
multiplication table by heart! It is absurd. They have no hearts. Nor have
they minds. They are but dumb muscle, animated by hunger and fear.
They fear for their bottoms; their abjection is *bottomless*, hah! hah! But
I am no harsh master,' he added, for Margaret Sphery's face had visibly
reddened. 'The children have their jolly moments. If only you could see
their savage delight at Christmastide when Taskmaster tosses out the
oranges! Some tell me that to feed oranges to scalawags is like feeding

buttered toast to mice! I say: Hang the expense! Christmas comes but once a year. It can be said—' and here Tubbs lowered his voice yet again for full effect, 'that the children who toil for Tubbs are the only children in England who can actually *count on their oranges at Christmas*. I'll tell you what—we shall visit the factory at Grimswick, yes! I shall take you there. Then you shall see for yourself how shipshape the place is, how rosy-cheeked the rascals. You shall see how *noble* an edifice it is, yes, my dear Mrs. Sphery,' he said, 'and bless my heart, *beautiful*. I believe that you will be impressed. You will change your mind about me and my treatment of the little ones.'

Tubbs had not seen Grimswick himself for over a decade and he set out alone the very next day to assure himself all was in good order. True, the brick facade was as strong and as turreted as any royal keep, but the guts and grounds were a shambles and cholera had recently killed off one-third of the working force.

Tubbs had a chance to show his mettle; a handkerchief drenched in cologne and held before his face, he made his investigation. The lodgings had not been whitewashed, nor, I dare say, *washed* for years; the water supply was sporadic and yellow, the lavatory floor swimming with *immondices*. Refuse had accumulated in heaps and barrels in the basement, the attic, the closets, the yards. The bleaching and dyeing pits were not ventilated and in those ill-lit rooms where snarling children crouched like skeletal gnomes, Tubbs had to admit it was impossible to breathe. . . . The river beyond was a purple sludge in which unrecognisable gobbets floated like the tripe in a poorhouse broth.

Tubbs set off for town at once and informed himself about refuse removal; he hired men to dredge the river and so quicken the flow of water (and I dare say, even today, the filth is ever carried downstream to other towns and villages situated upon its banks). With plumbers Tubbs planned the thorough transformation of the sanitary system, hired no less than twelve robust drudges, a laundress (and bought new bedding and new linens) and carpenters, painters and gardeners, roofers; he set up an infirmary and hired nurses.

The stairs, splintered and hazardous, were torn down and rebuilt; traps were set in the attic for rats that navigated the walls constantly jabbering; the entire building was scrubbed down with lye; the kitchen and refectory remodeled. Tubbs hired a new kitchen staff and enlivened the menu: chicken soup, applesauce, boiled cabbage well buttered and bran porridge to be served daily (with a slab of salt cod and toast *with jam on Sundays!*). He saw to it that all these changes were made as swiftly as possible. The cost was tremendous but he knew Margaret Sphery was the one defective cog in his wheel and he was desperate to win her over. After four horrible days Tubbs left behind (and undoubtedly with much relief) the brute faces of carpenters and the pinched, ferrety faces of the orphans he despised: his hirelings.

The date of his return visit with Margaret Sphery decided upon, Tubbs inspected Grimswick again at which time, inspired, he had a little library installed and filled to the brim with red-bound books. This gave a homey character to the entrance. But he saw that three pits of stagnant water of a most diabolical colouration remained to the east beside a copse which was dying.

The sick trees were cut down for firewood and the pits filled with gravel and soil. Flowering bushes were planted next, although these did not survive (and indeed the area remains disconsolately barren). Lastly gravel was laid down over the dirt road which led to Tubbs's Grimswick Dyeworks and an enormous bucket of gardenias set out beside the entrance. (All these changes cut deeply into Tubbs's profits for the year, moneys he planned to sink into pyramids.)

Margaret Sphery's visit to Grimswick proved a great success. Mother was dumbstruck, had to admit that the place was not the 'sinister Hell-hole' her friend had described. Tubbs had orchestrated the day in such a way that just as they arrived the imps were partaking of their tea. Exceptionally, tarts had been provided, and ham sandwiches. The children, hand-picked, scrubbed, starched and rosy-cheeked, had been drugged into a contented silence. A matronly figure in white proffered Margaret Sphery a cucumber sandwich and a strawberry tart on a little china dish. Our mother was hungry and smiled at Tubbs for the first time. I believe her appetite proved ruinous.

To quote Tubbs's Oxford journals:

'Not long after the improvements, Grimswick was cited as a model of its kind and even the fearsome Twining was forced to agree, yet had the cheek to express bewilderment over the little library of "beautifully bound and *uncut* books of fairy tales which, I presume, were there for the benefit of illiterate children."

'You might infer that I behaved dishonestly,' he goes on to say, 'but I insist, with the transparency with which I manage all my affairs, that *love* precipitated the Grimswick metamorphosis, and who would deny that our most generous acts are spurred on by love?'

The following week Margaret Sphery was racked by an imperious vomiting and diarrhea. The symptoms were recognised at once by the family doctor who kept her in seclusion until the danger of infection had passed and who bade us boil our milk, meat, vegetables and fruit. Miraculously no one else was taken sick, but our mother never fully recovered. That robust, willful woman whom Radulph criminally describes in his journal as 'nettlesome, meddlesome and acidulous,' was confined ever after to a chaise longue loosely wrapped in flannel dressing gowns open at the throat and wrists (for she was easily chaffed and could not bear constrictions of any kind), swilling soups of seeded grapes, sugared toast and white wine, and staring into the eyes of her outsized walking stick. But before the cholera had devastated her (and so our household) Margaret Sphery had told her husband that despite previous evidence to the contrary, having seen Grimswick with her own eyes, she had to admit that although the man was a pretentious boor, he was not the knave he appeared. Our mother thereafter hushed and invalid, Tubbs was a regular guest to dinner and each time he came he brought Angus Sphery's daughters gifts of Italian candied pears, Egyptian dates and Spanish nougat.

It was during this period that Radulph Tubbs spoke to Angus Sphery for the first time about his projected voyage.

'One day soon I shall confront the great stone tetrahedrons of Egypt,' he told my father with his habitual pomposity; 'I have been told that the landscape all about them is perfectly smooth and flat! Imagine that: *perfectly smooth and flat!*'

My father, egged on by Tubbs's enthusiasm, dared express his conviction that the Egyptian hieroglyphs that once covered the pyramids from top to bottom were the keys to an objective reality which was that of *Eden prior to the Fall*. He next pulled a well-thumbed folio from a shelf and lay it open. Swiftly gained by giddiness, Radulph Tubbs gazed down at asps, severed legs, owls and royal figures throned upon emptiness.

'These figures are of such magical potency,' Angus Sphery told Tubbs, 'that it suffices to trace one with the finger and utter the secret name of Isis for the thing signified to spring into being.' He hesitated. 'Unfortunately the secret name of Isis is lost.'

Radulph Tubbs was thrust into a rare agitation.

'The text!' he breathed. 'Can you read it?'

'I can,' Angus Sphery replied. 'It is from the *Book of the Dead* and is called "The Chapter of Giving Air to Nu in Khert-Neter."

> *Hail, thou God Tomu, grant thou unto me the*
> *sweet breath which dwelleth in thy nostrils!*
> *I am the Egg which is in the Great Cackler . . .*
> *I live, it liveth; I grow, I live, I snuff the air.*
> *I am the God Utchā-aābet, and I go about*
> *his egg. I shine. Hail dweller among the*
> *celestial food. Hail dweller among the beings*
> *of Lapis Lazuli.*

'Lapis Lazuli refers to the Ether,' said Angus Sphery. 'I named my eldest daughter after this text.'

'Ah!' Enthusiasm flamed through Tubbs's soul. 'How the wind of Science inflates the mind!'

In his memoir, Radulph describes the continuation of his extended courtship as follows:

'That afternoon at dinner, Etheria tossed a paper dart in my direction. The missive landed in my lap and generated a tumescence which troubled me throughout the meal. I unfolded the paper and read:

'"I fear I cannot compete with your friend Mr. Dodgson, I replied evenly, although envy still gnawed at my heart.

"'No one can!" Memory agreed.

"'Memory. You are being rude." Angus Sphery admonished his daughter sadly. The brat stuck her knuckle into her mouth and savagely nibbled a wart.

"'Etheria says Tubbs has the imagination of an oyster," Memory mumbled behind her fist loud enough for me to hear. I saw her sister blush and racked my brains. And then inspiration hit, God only knows from where, like a chunk of ice from the sky:

"'Why is a Spanish onion like *King Lear*?" I'd heard the riddle as a child, o so many, many years before. Memory frowned:

"'We've not heard that one." But Etheria smiled pensively. I had pleased her. O God in Heaven I had pleased the superb creature. Her great violet eyes swept the ceiling before alighting with a curious intensity upon my own. She shook her head. Memory grunted:

"'He has us stumped," and kicked the table leg. *O daughter of Eve and Isis*, I thought, devouring the adolescent with my eager eyes, *may you always be stumped this easily*. I said:

"'Because it will make you cry." Etheria was confused; I believe the tone of my voice may have perplexed her.

"'*Tragedy!*" burst Memory. "*Onions!*" Etheria nodded gravely and began to scribble something down on another piece of paper. "Now she's one for you"—said Memory, "and if you lose, you must give her whatever she asks. That's rule number one!"

"'Whose rule?" I asked.

"'Our rule!" Memory stared at me stubbornly, elbows on the table, her fists propped beneath her chin.

"'I shall give her whatever she wants," I said.

"'My daughters are impossible," said Angus Sphery, caressing Etheria's hair. She leaned and gently kissed her father on the ear. From a distant room I heard their mother whistle: a high, shrill piping tore through the air. Another dart sailed across the table.

This time it struck me in the face.

Ever eating, all devouring; never sated, all destroying, Never finding full repast, 'till I EAT THE WORLD at last.

I was lost. The housemaid pressed more trifle upon me. Somewhere

Margaret Sphery whistled again.

"*Death*," I said. "Death. *Death* . . . Yes! I know it is Death. It can only be Death!" Etheria looked bewildered. Memory shouted:

"'You've *lost!* It's TIME! Time's the usual answer. Papa." She turned to her father. "What do you think? They *are* dreadfully alike," she admitted.

"'Time's better." The butterfly collector dipped into his trifle dreamily. "Death eats only the organic . . ."

"'Well then, she's *won!*" Etheria nodded at her sister and smiled at me sweetly. "And now Tubbs must give her whatever she asks!"

"'Indeed." I stroked my moustache and, fearing my gaze betrayed my intolerable, irrepressible desire, blew my nose. My erection rattled in my trousers like an angry snake. With a flourish Etheria thrust her dart. I captured the missive in midair.

"'*The chimera*," I read aloud. "*And her pup.*"

"'*Etheria!*" Her father was scandalized. "You have gone too far! I am mortified." He turned to me apologetically. "The child has no idea as to its value."

"'Chimera? *What* chimera? I have no chimera!"

"'Yes you *do!*" Memory scolded. "A wonderful chimera *in your jade cabinet.*" She sat back triumphantly. Again her sister blushed. Her face was so soft and pink that for one mad instant I thought of biting into it.

'All at once I recalled the piece, a convoluted lump of pagan extravagance the colour of raw suet.

"'She shall have it."

"'It's not for *her!*" The precocious brat bounced up and down in her chair with excitement. "But for Papa! It is to be his birthday, Saturday. He wants it badly." From somewhere Margaret Sphery whistled three times; to my surprise no one stirred.

"'Memory—" my host's embarrassment amused me.

"'Etheria won it fairly!" Memory leapt from her chair and placed a hearty kiss on the divine sister's cheek.

"'So she has," I agreed.

"'The chimera is priceless," Angus Sphery protested weakly.

"'The jewel of my collection," I agreed, and lifting my glass said: "To

Etheria, that other chimera. . . ." The child blushed scarlet and stared at her hands which were white, tapered and cool-looking.'

Here I must cut in. Because it was precisely at that moment that an incident occurred that was to further aggravate our mother's precarious sanity. (All things in this world are precarious, but sanity, I am convinced, is the most precarious of all.) Tubbs suddenly threw his glass across the room and, screaming, brought his fist down with a clatter upon an unusually large insect that had made its way into the room, smashing it to bits. As we all feared, the thrashing particles proved, most regrettably, to be those of Margaret Sphery's beloved walking stick.

The following Saturday as promised, Tubbs brought the chimera wrapped in its scrap of silk. His memoir describes the rest:

'Etheria was sitting in a wicker chair in the garden. For several moments the jade was passed from hand to hand. When it reached Etheria she placed it first against her cheek as if to warm it or to feel its warmth, and then in the crease between her thighs. Her thighs were unusually lean and long, like those of a boy. I was deeply moved.

'Thereafter I followed her discreetly, spent many irritating hours in the park just to catch a glimpse of her feeding the ducks with crusts from her apron pocket. And more than once, to my infinite displeasure, I caught sight of her navigating the water lilies of Cherwal with that milk-fed nanny, that scholar and idler Charles Dodgson in boating flannels and stuttering so badly the air was full of foam!'

This is a blatant lie! Dodgson *never* stuttered in our company. And I shall take this occasion to inform the reader that although it is true as a small child I oft nibbled my warts, I was nothing like the pest he describes with such viciousness!

His dislike of me at the time was palpable and already I did my best to hate him back. My vanity was wounded by his preference for Etheria and if I sucked his nougat, I mocked him shamelessly as soon as his back was turned.

CHAPTER
5

Etheria's beauty at seventeen was such that Angus Sphery feared, above all else, that his daughter, a creature of air and light, might, by an imprudent elopement, confront the squalor of the world. By this time he knew Radulph Tubbs's adoration was sincere; this, Tubbs's maturity and wealth, convinced Father that he was the ideal husband.

'However,' Radulph wrote, 'omens unknown to me, dark rings around the fairy moons of Etheria's childish fancies, continued to warn her against me and our engagement was broken twice before she consented to be my wife—a decision hastened when her mother's malady took a queer and violent turn. In an excess of bloodlust, anger or despair, she tore off the heads of her paired Australian finches with her teeth and spat them out upon the carpet. Etheria discovered the mess and buried it in a sewing basket which the cat grubbed up and brought to the attention of the maid. Upon learning of the matter, Angus Sphery summoned me.

'"Radulph," he said (and he was weeping), "you must take my Etheria away as soon as possible."

'At the wedding ceremony Etheria was so frail, so pale, so thin, I thought she'd break beneath the burden of my gaze.'

In guise of a honeymoon, Tubbs, prince among merchants, took Etheria across Britain and Wales to trumpet the outspread of his holdings. As she traveled from site to site, Etheria noted that the dog had marked his territory with a stench, and that his gentleman's airs were a sham.

Tubbs was all greed and gravy: three puddings at the pudding course, his fingers perpetually redolent of Stilton, and his *favoris* of maraschino jelly. In bed he indulged 'Sir Reverence'—are all wives, one wonders, such intimate witnesses to their husband's corporality?

The only time Etheria saw Tubbs *happy* was during the contemplation of his smokestacks and his profits. Imagine him taking his ease in a hideous tasselated chair, a slice of cheese in one fist, a pen in the other and in his mouth the black chimney of a *Chivas*. He calculates, he ciphers up, he recounts, he double-checks, he beams: each farthing turned comes up two, the pounds sterling are rolling in—a tidal wave! And his vision is truly pharaonic. Radulph Tubbs will be the Sovereign Sultan of carbon monoxide! His love of smoke brings Nero to mind. One day the planet will be circled in a dark ring of Chivas Havannah!

Sometime during the first months of her marriage Etheria wrote in the secret little book she kept:

> *My husband loves substantial things;*
> *he slavers to hear the lunch-bell ring.*
> *He sups on a steady flow of cash*
> *and savours the sweat of the working class.*

Which reminds me of Feather the butler's monkeyshines. Feather had printed a set of calling cards in the name of Mr. Marx. From time to time he would bring one to Tubbs on a silver dish:

'Marx? Marx? Who the devil is this fellow?' Tubbs growls. 'Never heard of him!'

'Indeed, Sir, you are bound to, sooner or later.' Feather answers with such a straight face Etheria is forced to leave the room and stifle her laughter with a bolster.

At this time the New Age had an unusual garden and whenever she possibly could Etheria lifted the key from the pantry and slipped out to spend a stolen hour there. Skirting the cook's vegetables, she crossed a little bridge and entered an overgrown pergola, treacherous of thorny bramble and smelling strongly of roses. The pergola stretched on for twenty yards or so when all at once the path, steeped in sunlight, metamorphosed into a picture pavement. Here in variegated pebbles were portrayed Narcissus staring into the treacherous pool, Aescalapius, Icarus, Arachne and—nearly concealed beneath a creeping vine—Perseus, my sister's favourite, his little wings bravely beating the air as he held the Gorgon's severed head by its hissing hair. The monster's blood seeded serpents that danced on their tails in the manner of creatures in Wonderland.

To the east this pavement led to a sundial propped on the back of a curious tortoise as clawed as any griffin and blue with verdigris, and to the west a grotto built of seaside rocks, riddled by the rude fingers of barnacles. A marble love seat crouched within it, goblinlike and green. In the shadows brooded a very fat toad, which upon each of Etheria's repeated intrusions swelled with indignation before scrabbling off.

Etheria came here to 'distill magic,' to gaze upon Aescalapius the owl winking from within a forest of pale, pink mushrooms, to spy upon a living snake hunting in the grass. Hidden in the grotto she wrote in her diary:

Dodgson once told me that the centre of the eye is called a 'pupil' because if one looks into another's eyes one sees oneself reflected in miniature, just like a puppet. As I sit here, I think that when I look into my husband's eyes *that is how I see myself.*

And now the time has come for me to quote extensively from Tubbs's memoir, pretentious and scandalous as it may be, for it is, I believe, honest, and describes in depth certain occurrences and attitudes that precipitated my sister's vanishment.

'Our lives together, Etheria's and mine, began far from the thick and thunder of life here at the New Age, a house like a solid mountain of granite which casts an eminently respectable chill all about Bear's Lane. I had the plumbing installed myself; drains and running water are the modernist's answer to Nature's despotic doctrine of Necessity.

'The New Age has three storeys, windows of leaded glass, a roof of blue slate, a front door of solid oak five inches thick, a gracious, granite-paved vestibule, three stairwells, decorative plasterwork on all the ceilings of such tortuous relief they demand the constant attentions of a sweeper, rare carpets and that confounded jade cabinet, now empty, which at the time of my marriage brimmed with jade the colour of spinach, of stagnant water and mutton fat, of bone and dead fish. I could not foresee that Etheria, as had her father, would take to these. Within the week I found her sprawled out upon the carpet fast asleep, the entire collection set down beside her in an undecipherable pattern. The ugly things had become her toys.

'This took place in the west room and the sun setting just behind my wife's blonde head illuminated the jade so that those inanimate objects appeared to throb and pulse in the heated air, the translucent and airy clues, perhaps, to the mystic knot of Etheria's heart.

'I saw that an owl and a bear lay near her sweet face, and a lavender unicorn . . . a griffin, turtles, tigers and a rabbit appeared to be tempted by her outstretched hand. In one fist she held a monkey, and at her feet a pair of carp lay locked in a tense embrace—symbols, Angus Sphery had informed me, of connubial bliss.

'I thought the time had come for me to enter her; not until that hour had I dared. Her cries caused me to weep with exasperation, to spend myself too swiftly; I lost patience with her reticence; her anger put me out of temper; I tore her dress; her hair caught in the ruby at my cuff; I could not help myself: you see it was the sight of Etheria abandoned in sleep, her heart visibly beating beneath the fine stuff at her breast—and all that weird clutter of hieratic phoenixes, dragons and peonies metamorphosed into playthings and shimmering in that gorgeous light, as soft and mysterious as my beloved's skin and hair—that forced me upon her, that forced my mouth to hers to stifle her muted cries; that left the infamous marks of my famishment upon her breasts, her neck, her thighs.

'If I choose to tell my story it is because with age I have come to consider that all men are one man; that my story might have been yours, and yours mine. Are we not all ruled by the same treacherous emotions, the same pitiable vanities, the same blindness? Have we not all ruled our wives, our concubines, our children with tyranny more or less disguised; do we not live our lives with the laborious futilities, the devastating shortsightedness of moles?

'I have known men who by a concerted effort of the will transformed their hearts and proceeded with a clarified vision and even brilliancy.

Now I know that Charles Dodgson was, after all, such a one. It is too late for me, however, to undo what I have done. And if, as I now fear, I am but a reflection of all other men, darkness will continue to gather and evil to cloak the world as a film of opacified matter.

'These days my movements are limited by cataracts, other infirmities. Few distractions disturb the process of conjuration, of what has been: a wasted, wasteful life. Above all a sinful life. Yes—although godless, I have come to believe in Sin; I am a sinner, and it is Sin which has given this body of mine its almost unbearable weight. The gravity that grounds me is of my own making. . . .

'Etheria enshrined at the New Age with her toys, fairy books and puzzles, I set about to acquire the Other End, a Gothic horror appendaged to mine and for which I paid an outrageous price. During the demolition I ignored several petitions attesting to the hovel's significance and instead enquired after architects. For weeks rosebuds and wags attempted to impose their "taste" upon me. At last came Baconfield the Fundamentalist, whose refreshingly functional vocabulary included such concrete jewels as "ultra-Spartan."

'I described the nursery he was to build for the son Etheria would bear me. I explained that I wanted my son to grow into a citizen of the coming century, to admire from childhood not the flimsy, transient stuff of nature, nor a dead God and His overcharged cathedrals, but the sights and sounds of operative steam engines, life-sized.

'Baconfield, who threw himself gladly into the spirit of the thing, proposed a "Temple to Industry and Infancy." We saw eye to eye, and speaking of eyes, he proposed that the inscrutable visage of his windowless building (all light supplied artificially so that my son should not look out and dream upon the street or garden but upon the wonderful machines thumping and pounding and whistling away within) be tempered by a motto writ in pink granite upon the grey, a motto which seized my mind instantaneously and which Baconfield approved enthusiastically:

GIVE ME STEAM, THEN SHALL I DREAM

'Baconfield abhorred stairways, "crude ladders disguised." Said he:

"Many an innocent has smashed his skull in the bosom of his family."
(Baconfield himself had suffered such a misadventure as an infant.)
"Our nursery must be level with the ground. Your little son shall
toddle from exhibit A to Z without mishap. He shall enter from the back
court cobbled smooth and broad and straight; from the arched entrance
an austere clock tower will be visible, its severe arms and brass bells
continuously beating time." (As it still does! Time lies stretched out,
bruised and bleeding all about me!)

'I savoured Baconfield's vision as if it were my own; indeed it very
nearly was. "Each exhibit will be kept behind glass," he continued; "the
infant will ambulate through glass corridors, beneath a luminous glass
ceiling. The motors will be activated by bodily heat—you intend to hire
a full-time mechanic?"

"'Yes!" I replied enthusiastically.

"'Splendid!" Baconfield approved. "I shall design his uniform in
tune with the harmony of the whole. The nanny's as well. Gay colours;
austere lines. A yellow suit and cap with turquoise piping: the iron struts,
the pediments, the banded masonry shall all be turquoise and canary
yellow; all the other fixings brass. The mechanic will be obliged to polish
the brass.

"'In the large, circular amusement arena, the infant will have the
platonic solids to play with, a set of cubes of my own design and a
miniature in lead of the Liverpool-Manchester Line."

'I was greatly elated by Baconfield's visit. Before he left I asked him
to come up with a plan for the facade of the New Age so that the two
structures, new and old, would be wedded as one. Then I went to fetch
Etheria who was mooning in her rooms.

'She was standing before the splendour of her mirror, her unbound
hair sweeping to her boyish hips. She was wearing a satin gown, very
becoming. She shuddered when she saw my reflection.

'I bade her come with me for a brief ride in the country. She frowned
yet acquiesced with a silent nod of her head. Her manner provoked
me. I knew she had character, and yet she had of late shown me only
an obstinate spiritlessness.

'And now for another confession: *carriages have always stimulated
me.* Not only the sight of the horses' raw and oversized particulars and

those great, black backsides, but the cab itself, its smell of leather, its intimacy, the way it lurches and rolls from side to side, the churn and ferment of the wheels. One pulls the little velvet curtain and *presto:* magically the world is eclipsed. One is precipitated into limbo, a neverland wherein all the rules are one's own, an orchestrated chaos.

'I waited until we were far from town to draw the curtains. And then I threw myself upon my wife. Although she surely had a voice, she did not scream but, battering me with her fragile fists, uttered low guttural sobs, like those of a captured doe. Straddling her waist I pinned Etheria's hands behind her and then, pushing her up against the seat, her unbound hair pulled taut beneath her, spread her thighs with my arms and pressed my face to her sex which burned, I swear, beneath my lips. Etheria's struggles ceased and to her surprise as much as mine, and to her infinite shame and anger, her pleasure exploded, cascading in violent spasms against my tongue, my teeth—tearing from my own depths a sob and a dark longing as I had never known. Then as she wept I crushed her damp body to me and saw to my horror that I held in my hand a clump of her hair!'

CHAPTER
6

Each instant she could in that closeted, tasselated, somber house,
Etheria searched within herself for those infinite spaces where her
soul might freely wander. She considered that the nature of solitude had,
since her marriage, abruptly changed. She thought that the solitude of
peace resonates and rebounds and is not, properly speaking, solitude
at all. Whereas Tubbs's house of routines and ubiquitous servants and
sudden, dark eroticism imposed a solitude of an entirely different order.

For the first time in her life she felt impoverished. As she expressed
it in her secret book, *she no more carried the world within her*. A door
had been shut, and a window; it was as if she had been gagged and
trussed and abandoned in an empty, airless attic. She wanted to shout
for help and suffered from her voicelessness. She dared not inform us
of her plight—our father was old and I but twelve.

Yet, the New Age contained keys to the only world that really
mattered to her: that of the imagination. These keys, as you have seen,
were the garden and the jade cabinet. When the jade bestiary was set
down on the carpet on an imaginary journey, it was as if Etheria had left
the house. She was following Marco Polo's routes from Venice to Samar-
kand, Karakoum to Baghdad. Dreaming in the garden grotto she was
transported to the ascending terraces and terra cotta faces of southern
Italy; she sat beside the peculiar fountains of France and lost herself in
the labyrinths of Portugal. She had read that in Cyprus the horizon was
violet-hued and golden green; above all it was very far away.

When Etheria was in the garden, she felt like *Peau d'Ane*, her donkey's skin cast aside. Here she peeled the world down to its bare essentials and waited for Adonis. The butler came instead!

She had been sitting in the shade for an entire afternoon; already it was evening. As Etheria followed Feather back to the New Age, she saw the world in reverse, saw the backside of Baconfield's idealised palace looming in silhouette against the sky's paler ink, its gaping central arch and one blind eye—an *oeil-de-boeuf* fitted out with black glass.

Already the skeleton of the clock tower—symbol of Radulph's aspirations for his potential son—rose eight storeys to a roof as pointed as a dervish's cap. Beyond that terrible needle the sky hung moonless and swarmed with stars. The sight of those innumerable beacons did not soothe her, rather their excessive quantity seemed suspect, as if Tubbs's vanity had tainted Heaven:

> *I was startled by a thought,*
> *sinful to the extreme, that*
> *God Himself might be very*
> *like my husband: brutal,*
> *greedy and vain.*

Tubbs, for whom the day's four meals were perceived as the precious cogs of a clockwork, was enraged when his young wife appeared late with twigs in her hair. He reached out, apparently with the intention to strike her, just as the housekeeper, carrying a silver bell, materialised to ask with ill-concealed temper if her master and mistress intended to sit down to supper. A rich smell wafted through the hall and Radulph, forgetting his anger, took his wife's arm and led her into the dining room. Thus did Appetite spare her a slap: turtle soup, parslied tongue, three heaping servings of raspberry trifle. From behind a curtain, did she see Feather wink?

Once, as Etheria rode with her husband in his fearful carriage, she caught a glimpse of Mr. Dodgson leading a little girl into a comfit shop. Etheria felt such a pang of nostalgia for the child she had been that she pleaded with Tubbs to have the carriage turned about and directed to church college. She longed to see Angus Sphery's study, that enchanted playroom where as small children we had spent so many delightful hours among the butterflies and bottled bats. As Tubbs paced the lawns mauling a Chivas with his lips and teeth and causing great puffs of smoke to rise above him in the air, Etheria took the key she always kept with her from a little beaded purse and turned the lock.

Father's cabinets were as ordered and silent as they had always been. The old orang's familiar figure surged in friendly greeting from his glittering glass case. To see those extravagantly various structures, even dead, centred her, made her joyous. Here Etheria always felt she had been given a glimpse into the loving, cunning mazes of God's own mind, a mind which, in Father's study, and far from the New Age, appeared playful.

I recall that when we were little Etheria had expressed the wish to *see the intimate structures of a single feather at the moment of conception. Rather like a snowflake or a crystal of salt, she supposed, transparent, a thing of air.* She pondered: *From the moment the Creator perceived the possibility of a thing to its actual realisation, was there a sort of spontaneous ladder or bridge? If one could see God's thoughts, if they could somehow be mapped, just what would one see?*

One day, long ago, when we 'played at questions' with Mr. Dodgson, Etheria asked: *But what does it look like when God thinks?* Inspired, he answered without hesitation: 'A spiral staircase.' Surely he was teasing, and yet at the time we thought: what a curiously exhilarating idea!

That same afternoon Dodgson took us to the Museum of Natural History to see the staircase there—all done in iron filigree and painted white. Climbing to the third storey was like scaling the spine of a perpendicular whale.

Dodgson, at the top of his form, regaled us with endless variations upon the theme of the spiral. I recall a story about a greedy snake that swallowed a clock spring, and a curious tornado that managed to encapsulate itself in an empty shell . . .

Upon returning home with Tubbs, Etheria rifled through her things until she found her own empty comfit tin of long ago—an especial pretty one with a picture of young lovers seated together in a beautiful garden. It had been filled with sugarcoated aniseeds from France. Dodgson had told her that nuns had made the comfits, and that their clothes smelled of anise, as did the air they breathed. Etheria wanted to know if their hair smelled of anise as well; he said he thought not, as they had none—it was shaved off, you see; but he supposed their *eyelashes* did!

One evening when Feather went up to Etheria with her tea he saw that she had been weeping. To cheer her he took up all the lace antimacassars from the chairs and made himself a pair of ludicrous epaulettes and a cockade. He also did a cunning trick with two silk handkerchiefs, one scarlet and one turquoise green. He placed them on his knees and asked Etheria to choose. She chose the scarlet and, as she was bid, placed it beneath a pillow. Feather muttered a magical word and clapping his hands, pulled the scarlet handkerchief from the air. Etheria ran to the pillow and upon taking it up discovered a gilded rope and a heart made of barley sugar. The scarlet handkerchief had vanished. But when Feather tore a tassel from a chair and stuck it beneath his nose her heart constricted for she heard Tubbs's carriage thundering through the gate. The clocks slowed down, or so it seemed, and a chill settled over the house.

Feather was a tiny Irishman, his face as naked as an infant's—one trusted him entirely. The man was well-formed, his proportions neat and features charming. Whenever Tubbs was away Etheria followed Feather around the house and looked on as he polished the silver or brushed Tubbs's extensive wardrobe of beaver coats and hats.

Feather did the queerest magic with shoe-polish tins and polishing rags: he could make them vanish altogether at will or, with a twist of the wrist, transform them into puppet cats and mice. And the stolen tassel appeared throughout the house in the oddest places. . . . For instance, once as the serving girl stood at Etheria's shoulder with a platter of broiled fish, she saw it concealed among the parsley garnish. That was the day the spectral Baconfield was for dinner and Tubbs had three puddings served in his honour shaped like Kheops, Khephren, and Mycerinus. Large puddings these were, banquet-size (Tubbs's joke), but being made mostly of cornstarch and water, utterly tasteless.

As they ate Tubbs and his architect discussed a plan to raze the garden. Tubbs had a terror of the grotesque and the fanciful—he abhorred anything that intimated the extraordinary. He admired pyramids because they were solids and geometric shapes; he hated anything convoluted. My theory is he hated and feared the world's feminine aspect—that is to say, anything folded, concealed, creased. Etheria's darling grotto gave him the willies. He wanted a *perfectly smooth* courtyard so that his infant son would always be visible to the naked eye and thus never in mischief. The grotto was dark and it was damp; worse: it was hidden from view. The sundial was redundant as the house contained no less than twelve clocks; the pagan pictures just the sort of thing to pervert a little boy's imagination.

Etheria, breathing hard, penned her husband a note and passed it to him.

'I did not ask your advice,' Tubbs snarled as Baconfield huddled over his uneatable slice of Egypt. Tubbs read:

Should I ever have a child, I should want, above all things, for it to see those pavement pictures, and to dream upon them entire afternoons together. If you remove the sundial and the grotto + the picture pavements, there will be nothing left to keep me here.

Etheria was trembling so that all the silver on the table rattled dreadfully like some small army carrying swords and shields to battle.

'Your *vows* will keep you here, I suppose,' said Tubbs. He added cynically: 'And your father's peace of mind. *Surely!*' he erupted with sudden laughter, 'a wife has never left her husband because of a quarrel over a sundial! Tell me—' he turned to his embarrassed guest, attempting to pass the whole thing off in jest, 'do *you* ever lose *your* temper?'

'I have no wife—' Baconfield began, causing Radulph Tubbs to roar with laughter.

Soon their lives were punctuated by the cries of workmen and the sound of their hammers. The air about the house was so thick with dust that looking out the window Etheria could not see the street. Impressive cumulations of granite, grey and pink, towered in the mud of the future courtyard.

'In those days,' Radulph writes, 'the demons of architecture snapped at my heels and the demons of my own unbridled vanity. In my fool-hardy quest for modernity I had razed all the trees. The cobbled court would forever be clear of leaves (a firm believer in *clarity*, I abhorred *obscurity*—except during sexual intercourse); all summer the sun would scour the place free of bacteria and pests.

'Despite Etheria's protests I hired men to remove the garden so that the courtyard should extend unimpeded from behind both structures, the new and old, as sober as any temple terrace. I assured Etheria who was nervously weeping (a habit she had acquired by the third week of our marriage) that once the nursery and courtyard were completed I would have trees brought over in *tubs*. At this she burst into hysterical, if silent, laughter. Always unable to bear strong emotions, especially coming from women, I soundly slapped that lovely woman's face. We were in the library; I saw that she had been toying with the jade. Upon an ebony table a procession of aberrations headed for a bone white *sampan* dipping upon a green froth. Was she playing at Noah's ark? I asked, all at once touched by her insistent childishness. When her beautiful face flushed with fear and anger, I was myself so enraged I took up a griffin and hurled it from the room. It sailed through the air and shattering a window, tumbled to the street where workmen were unloading turquoise tiles. Etheria turned as if to run from the room, her hair beating the air like a flame. I grabbed her arm and shouted:

'"If you want to toy with jade, you shall!" Dragging her to a writing table, and taking a small key from my pocket, I opened a drawer and removed an object hidden there: a phallus, life-sized, and carved of deep green jade.

'Etheria screamed—for the first and last time her voice pierced the air—and again attempted to flee. Savagely I pulled her down. As we fell together, we collided into the table, which capsized. The jade animals, like the fallen zodiacs of Heaven, spilled to the floor.

'I remember how I thrust the object into the very depths of her, how I invaded her as she had never dreamed possible, possessed her so unnaturally that had it lasted a moment longer, surely her heart would have broken. Spent, I kneeled, then stood. Etheria lay in ruins at my feet. Thus for the third time, I had made her mine.

'From that day on she was cold but pliant; it appeared that she had come to her senses. Nevertheless, to punish her I saw her little, kept her locked within the house, and spent my time overseeing the construction with Baconfield who graciously expounded upon the differences between columns, pillars, and posts; friezes and frets, the flying and the hanging buttress, the Roman and the Romanesque, tetragrams and tetragons, pergolas and porticoes, the socle and the pedical. And we discussed other possibilities and future plans: my own three pyramids, an obelisk in the centre of Nottingham Market, a model cotton mill based on Hatshepsut's mortuary temple, a visit to Egypt. Already I was grateful to the man for extending not only my holdings but my vocabulary. Thanks to Baconfield I was able to speak of "asymmetrical harmony" and "solemn orchestration," and to dream of that country where massive monuments of granite rose above the flatlands poised upon eternity.

'"We shall sleep on the sands of Ghîzeh," Baconfield foamed a little at the mouth in his excitement. "The goddess Nut's arched body our only roof! We shall awaken to the splendour of the rising sun as it strikes the flanks of the Great Pyramid."

'When, but a few months later, Etheria vanished forever in thin air like a puff of smoke, I was astonished. The blow to my self-esteem was boundless. Even now my heart reverberates with a tremor I trace to the abandonment. My heart has never been the same, nor, for that matter, has my mind. As far as I knew no female of the Tubbs line had ever behaved so shabbily. Not the mop-washers nor the fishwives my ancestors had taken for their own. A laughingstock, I stormed into Angus Sphery's house to raise a tempest; Margaret Sphery's shrill birdcalls, whistles, and hoots assailed us from a proximitous room.

'The old professor collapsed, ashen and shaken, into his chair. As I prepared to leave, Memory came running and, catching sight of her prostrate father, demanded to know what on earth was the matter.

'"Your sister is a slut, *that* is the matter!" I said, "and a thief and a vagabond." Slamming the front door behind me I collided into Dodgson, who was carrying a paper kite. In the blindness of my anger and despair I tore it from his hands and before the man's astonished gaze, trampled it to shreds.'

Before ending this chapter, I wish to add that Baconfield was obsessed with geometry and with Pythagoras in particular, who had postulated that the universe is made of ten equiradial circles extending from four— at the base—to one—at the top, the whole forming a species of pyramid:

The gaps between those circles perplexed Pythagoras who solved the problem by overlapping the circles to make a

honeycomb: . But those *gaps* continued to plague Baconfield, who claimed that the cosmos, its skeleton hopelessly porous, was bound to collapse sooner or later. Baconfield's panic infected Tubbs so that from the time Baconfield entered Tubbs's life, he could not sleep and the solidity of the Palace to Industry and Infancy, the substantiality of bricks and stones and mortar, became an obsession. That and Etheria's apparent sterility.

CHAPTER
7

Back to Tubbs's Oxford memoirs, if briefly. Despite everything, I cannot help but be touched by them from time to time. It is clear that he suffered too, although it is also true that he brought his suffering about himself.

'My life has been one of absurdities and incongruities,' he begins, 'but also of incident, and, I hope, of interest. You will observe that I attempt to speak with entire candour and to strictly avoid any embellishment of the truth. For I have come to realise that truth is a serviceable thing. Etheria's dislike of me, if—I realize it now—*justified*, was also exceedingly wearisome.

'All this is distasteful and humiliating to the extreme. However, this confession is for no man's eyes but mine own, or rather, the better man I believe I have become, and for you, Memory, the one fleshly link that remains with the woman I adore. Truth is the great feature of the hour; you shall see that my story unfolds unhindered by vanity.' (Would that were true! But I must let Radulph speak unimpeded, and let the reader judge for himself.)

'In April the new building was near complete; already it stood stark and magnificent, dwarfing the street which, once sunny, had taken on a perceptible chill. Baconfield came daily to oversee the work. The edifice was unquestionably *modern* and even today I cannot help but be thrilled by the inscrutable power of its vast, windowless facade and steep, glimmering roof.

'That spring the gardens were swept away. Etheria's protests had ceased and she appeared calm throughout the entire procedure although, I know it now, it pained her unspeakably to hear the workmen sawing and tearing at the trees and bushes, the clatter of wagons carting away the shattered pergola, picture pavements, and grotto she had so adored. Her love for such rubbish was incomprehensible to me but no matter; Etheria loved and had I been a better man, I should have respected that. Nevertheless, to justify myself, I should add that the garden was grotesque. It was damp, it smelled of mold. One could not go anywhere near it without ruining one's shoes. Insects bred there in countless numbers and beastly birds—their excrement falling without warning through the air. It was but a childish fancy of Etheria's to go there and brood, yet perhaps with time she would have grown out of it. No sane woman would have wished to bring an innocent babe into such an intoxicating turmoil of chlorophyll. Surely Etheria would have come to perceive things thus. Simply: had I been patient, these garden squabbles which undermined our union could have been avoided.

'To continue: the vegetation, those grotesque antiquities, were removed and the empty expanse paved end to end in grey and pink granite to most decorative, yet sober effect. (The courtyard is as handsome as ever it was *but so silent!* No child has ever gladdened it with happy cries, after all.)

'As the last stones were being laid and the clock tower fitted with its clock—Oxford's largest to this day—Etheria and I drove to Angus Sphery's home for Sunday dinner. We were greeted by Memory shocking in pantaloons—she had been out riding a bicycle with Dodgson's brother Wilfred. (Such unseemly dress and behaviour has since become almost commonplace.) The old bug collector, shackled by a great weariness of mind, greeted his daughter with tear-soaked eyes.

'Over soup the conversation was hesitant and tense; I did my best to entertain my host by describing in detail the New Age's transformations. Sphery's remarks were unnervingly eccentric:

'"Now that you have removed the brambles, where in Heaven will the *bees go?*"

'"The bees are the least of my worries!" I laughed, and lifting my glass, proposed a toast to "your grandson's playground."

'"Etheria?" Angus Sphery turned to his daughter with an expression of pain and hope together. To my exasperation, Memory blurted out: '"There's no infant on the way, Papa!" and pressed his hand.

'Just then a thunderous crash resounded from the hall where a weighty collection of mounted Amazonian butterflies had been unwittingly torn from its nail by Margaret Sphery, who appeared panting and unassisted, her red eyes beaming forth from their purple sockets, her mouth screwed into a concentrated blister. Trembling on her feet she held on to picture frames and furniture as the housemaid stood too shocked to put down her platter of curry to assist her mistress. When Margaret Sphery abandoned her moorings and plunged headlong into the room, Etheria and her sister leapt up to catch her. But the madwoman flayed her long, silvery arms to chase them off and, perambulating like a bewitched windmill, approached the table, gasping for breath. I stood up and offered her my chair, apparently the very one she coveted, and seizing her firmly by her elbow, helped her to settle down—no easy task—for the chair was ponderous, with arms, and she all bones and uncannily tall as if her illness had grabbed her simultaneously by her ankles and her neck and stretched her spine.

'Sphery stumbled off to fetch another chair, the table settings were shifted as with a low animal sound, betwixt a purr and a growl, my mother-in-law held her face to my dish and lapped up sauce and chutney. Once she had done she began to moan.

'With a shaking hand, Angus Sphery made to caress her hair which was unbound and horribly tangled, but she shook her mane irritably and snarling, made to bite his hand. As Memory fell to her knees weeping and pleaded with Margaret Sphery's hems to "release our dear, sweet mother!" Etheria did the most unexpected thing: she reached into the air and pulled forth one scarlet and one turquoise handkerchief. At once the madwoman's face altered dramatically. Etheria next knotted the two pieces of silk together, rolled them into a tight wad which she hid in her left fist, and then, with a nod of her head, as if in communion with an invisible demon, pulled forth—not a scarlet handkerchief, nor a turquoise one, but instead *a gilded rope*. Memory stopped weeping, and the old man gasped. I, surely from some deep-seated intuition, grew angry. However, Margaret Sphery had ceased her jibberish and her slavering;

she looked on with the benign eyes of a child, her tortured mouth sweetly smiling, her eyebrows winging an expression gently quizzical—so that this weird domestic event was transformed into a celebration of sorts for everyone but myself—for I could not help but wonder *where* Etheria had learned her magic; the gilded rope, once laid about her mother's neck, had transformed itself into a garland of roses. With a worsening mood I erroneously concluded that the magic could be blamed upon Dodgson.

'And yet, I could not help but be seduced by my young wife's fantastical, unbridled imagination and her high animal spirits which had returned. Above all, I admired her pluck. It was a courageous act to perform upon the tawdry stage of her mad mother's bosom and knees (where now a white rabbit sat peacefully nibbling the stem of a freshly cut gardenia). Yet this is what Etheria did, with grace, and, as always, utterly without self-consciousness.

'As the curry cooled, as Memory's keen and contemptuous eyes were occupied elsewhere than the scrutiny of my person, as Angus Sphery, in the desert of his dotage, beamed in the unexpected oasis Etheria had provided him, more gilded ropes and rabbits and squares of silk and silver rings and blooming gardenias appeared and disappeared with the sound of leaves falling through the air. And in the mild light of the deepening afternoon, a certain flavour of unreality permeating everything, the exalted madwoman stilled and dazzled, the real space of Angus Sphery's dining room was transformed into an imaginary space. The imaginary had so imposed itself that I could not have told you what was "in" or "out," "here" or "there," "up" or "down." To steal Mr. Gladstone's phrase, it was as if the oscillating air was as full of alterable matter as an "egg is full of meat."

'Next Memory discovered a mango in each apron pocket, as did her unsteady father and myself. These were given to the cook to be sliced; we ate them for dessert. And it seemed far less terrible and strange when, as we returned to our food, Margaret Sphery sucked her fingers or listened to the reverberations of voices and music the rest of us could not hear. She seemed appeased, and when Angus Sphery reached out across the table to take her hand in his, she did not complain; indeed she may have smiled. Of that party I alone was devoured by discontent and envy. Etheria's sudden genius had deeply troubled me. I wanted to own her utterly, yet I knew enough to know that the gift of which I had just perceived a fitful glimpse *could not be owned, nor seized, nor even won.'*

CHAPTER
8

All this happened long ago. And it would never have occurred to me, I am certain, to write it down if Radulph Tubbs had not in his dotage brought me—from guilt or a true transformation of the spirit—his memoirs; had he not appeared, as a ghost from the past, with his sorry packet of papers, begging, like any wayward dog, forgiveness. The few years which had elapsed since Etheria's vanishment had not treated him kindly. He was weathered, worn; his hair was white. Yet in his eyes I saw a compelling sadness and his beautiful mouth, once marred by a permanent sneer, looked soft. A tremor plagued his lower lip.

Last night I had a dream of Radulph Tubbs in his youth and upon awaking realised that once again I had some backtracking to do. I beg my reader's indulgence; I am no writer, yet intend to tell my story as best I can, to be as 'linear' as possible. (Baconfield would approve of me!) Yet this morning it seems to me that the story webs and nets about. It is a fabric, not a simple thread. My father used to say: 'The memory is an anthill. How it swarms!'

I was eleven when they married and cannot help but recall that there was, and despite his pomposity, something about Radulph's almost caricatural virility that was exciting. In those days Radulph's greediness showed only in the high colour of his neck and face, and the robustness of his build. If later he was to become frankly obese, in the '60s he cut a handsome figure. I hated and feared him, I thought him ludicrous, and yet, I flirted with him shamelessly as little girls do, despising myself all the while because I knew that Tubbs was as Dodgson once described him: 'a gargoyle gyroscope.' But you see, in those days young girls did not see many men. They were all perceived as potential corruptors and masters. Men were the chimeras of all our nightmares, the horned snakes haunting our most secret pools; each and every virile male a potential Frog Prince, Vampire, Saviour. Except, I must add, for Dodgson. Dodgson was so different, so unlike the others! *He was like us:* he was Louisa Carolina—at heart a little girl!

Back to my story.

One morning in May, awakening to see his young wife's head sunk so deeply in its pillow she appeared to be dead, Radulph roused Etheria with an unusually gentle kiss and to her delight proposed a visit to the Saint Giles Fair. It was a glorious day, so golden that even Radulph had been transmuted by it.

'Let us breakfast at once!' he cried, and reaching for a bell-pull, rang urgently for sprats to be sent up directly. He watched, voraciously, as his bride, her cheeks flushed with the unexpected pleasure, slipped from bed to hide behind a lacquered screen to crouch unseen above a chamber pot. The musical sound of her flow so fired him he made to tear the screen away just as Etheria appeared, still damp with sleep and fragrant, as barefooted as any waif. Her beauty was such that Tubbs threw himself at her feet to kiss her ankles, then her knees. He had never fallen to the floor for a woman before, and his own behaviour startled them both.

Recall: this happened in the first weeks of their marriage and in those early days, whenever Radulph shewed Etheria a kindness she would express the spontaneous and affectionate side of her nature eagerly. This resiliency had much to do with my sister's youth; she still had the heart of a child which a night's sleep could refresh and renew. And Etheria admitted in her secret book that despite the violence done her, a tender word could set her heart to beating faster, her terror thwarted by desire or, perhaps, simply—the child's desperate need for affection. And, if he had rudely abused her, the jade phallus was as yet unknown to her.

Radulph had always distrusted spontaneity and shows of affection, especially from women; he often joked that he approved such behaviour from domestic dogs only. Yet here they were, both on their knees now, kissing as the lovers they were not and *for the first and last time.* All this was a dream which was to vanish.

'My gentle child,' he said, caressing her hair, transported. 'My own sweet child.'

As Radulph and Etheria embraced then, years ago on the morning of the Saint Giles Fair, a maid appeared behind the door, carrying a breakfast tray, and just behind her Feather, bearing yet another missive from the mysterious Mr. Marx. The smell of freshly broiled fish and bacon, and the sight of soft-boiled eggs fitted out like Turks in turbans, aroused other appetites. In no time Tubbs was buttering his rolls and sprinkling his eggs with pepper.

Having breakfasted, my sister and her husband set off on foot. She was lovely that day: light-footed, gay, mercurial—an Ariel! And Tubbs beside as black as any stovepipe in his silks and woolens, as swaddled as a mummy, as substantial as a side of beef.

Long before they reached the fair they could see the golden haze of kicked-up dust which hung suspended above the entire quarter. The air swarmed with distant voices and already smelled, faintly at first, of horse droppings and ginger beer.

Radulph continued to be unusually light-headed and was at his most charming. He had slept well the night before, he had eaten with appetite, and the morning's eager dalliance with his young wife had enlightened his spirits. But the air, thus far mild, was swiftly heating and Tubbs, a sausage in casing, began to feel uncomfortable. The moments in which Etheria may have actually enjoyed her husband's company were numbered. The crowd thickened and a swarm of students drunk on beer sent Tubbs colliding into a table set out with hot dishes of snails in pepper sauce. Before he could defend himself, the snail-seller was eagerly swabbing him down with a cloth which reeked of onions and as he stood sputtering beneath the creature's hands, a prankster made off with his hat.

A pack of dogs, crazed by the smell of toasting sausage, broke through the crowd just then, and their infernal yapping, joined by the shrill whistles of puppeteers and piemen, precipitated Tubbs into the arms of an Hindoo magician as he was vomiting a mouthful of smoke.

In a desperate attempt to save the day, Etheria plucked two orange tickets from a hawker's filthy fingers and pulled her husband after her into the dark, still recess of a tent which promised:

INCONGRUITIES, MYSTERIES

As soon as they entered the tent, Tubbs felt oppressed. An attendant pushed aside a heavy curtain which stank of ordure and they navigated a dimly lit space dwarfed by a large octopus in a glass aquarium. Its eyes were unnaturally human, and it stared at Radulph and Etheria with a desperate energy, all the while rubbing its vast, globular head against the glass, perhaps in an attempt to relieve some discomfort. If Etheria's eyes filled with tears, Radulph was thoroughly disgusted.

'It is a *fish*,' he told her. 'Fish have no feelings.'

The mollusk's keeper was of Tubbs's own mind and climbing upon a stool, prodded its head sharply with a stick. The octopus reacted with violence, slamming itself against the back wall of its tank and contracting into a tight ball, much as a wounded spider. Fearing for it, Etheria pressed her face and hands to the glass, but already Tubbs had seized her by the arm and was dragging her towards the next exhibit: a two-headed terrier asleep in his pen and twitching as he dreamed of two-headed foxes, perhaps. Appalled by the vision, Radulph attempted to pull Etheria back, but a crowd was pressing in behind them now and they were constrained to follow the exhibit's itinerary illuminated by a ponderously humped and bellied hawker carrying a lamp. They saw a lizard-man wearing nothing but a silver codpiece and a luxurious pair of mutton chops; a horned pig, its horn and hooves stained crimson; a woman who claimed four supernumerary nipples and who, for the price of an auxiliary ticket promised to remove her blouse; as they passed she flashed a smile and they saw, for one brilliant instant in the gloom, that all her teeth were made of gold. It came to my sister that these people and these creatures were very like the books of some lesser demon's library. She could see their bindings and read the titles, but she longed to know their stories, to chart their lives' maps. She wondered who the dog belonged to, and the pig—had they names? The woman coyly toying with the buttons of her blouse—had she a name? But there was not time, nor room for note-writing and anyway, it was too dark in the tent to write or to read.

Now they had come to the fair's one jewel: in a glass cage illuminated like the cavern of an enchanted dream, with thick glass cups of many colours brimming with oil, stood an uncommonly thin creature so frail one might have wondered that the weight of gravity did not snap her in two.

She was white, perfectly white, the colour of sour milk; so white she was almost blue. Her hair was white, and her eyebrows and lashes; her lips so pale as to be nearly invisible; her eyes were red, the colour of sour cherries.

She stood blazing in the firelight, shrunken and swollen in turn, mistress of one million shades, the innumerable phantom moths of shadow which inhabited the air she breathed. She was very small, under five feet, and she was standing stiffly in a dress of white brocade, once sumptuous, now threadbare and soiled. She looked impoverished, yet her peculiar eyes expressed a fixity of purpose, and the faint smile which informed her face was coloured by a bitter irony so black it caused Etheria to shudder.

Raising his lamp so that the prodigy appeared to catch fire in her silvery dress, the hawker informed the crowd that the *Hungerkünstler* had not eaten for two months. Etheria saw that her dress, fitted with whalebone, appeared to support its occupant, just as a chrysanthemum, poised upon its skinny wand, is secured by a hoop of wire. The tiny woman's head with its mane of frost was very like a full-blown blossom.

In the hushed silence—for the crowd had caught its breath—it became apparent that the *Hungerkünstler* was speaking, yet her speech was an incomprehensible droning, the sound of hornets swarming. The hawker explained that she was speaking the language of angels, was, in fact, speaking to angels. An uninterrupted stream of sacred syllables erupted night and day from the *Hungerkünstler*'s mouth.

'The *Hungerkünstler* lives on air and converses with angels'; these were the hawker's exact words.

Tubbs, who was about to pontificate that 'freak shows are proof that all artists are freaks and art an aberration,' stood as if stung. Etheria was struck by his corpulence and high colour; he looked, she thought, overripe and ready to fall. And then, with a second tremor of misgiving, she saw our father, Angus Sphery, standing isolated from the crowd and listening to the creature of bone with an uncommon intensity, his face illuminated, apparently by hope. The hawker then lowered his lamp, and ushered the crowd to the exit. Etheria and Radulph stood outside the tent for a time waiting for our father. When he appeared his eyes were wild.

'What if she is . . .' Angus Sphery sputtered, deeply moved, 'is . . . *authentic?* All my life . . .' He took his daughter's arm.

Soon the streets thinned and stilled and the day's smells and noises were left behind, its dust and press and curiosities. Angus Sphery rattled feverishly on:

'If I could discover the origins of language . . . I would know the origins of mankind. Mankind and . . . his myths! Simultaneously! The roots of the imagination and . . . *all its fruits!* The sciences, yes, and the arts. Because . . . Language is Imagination! Language is Memory! And the brain . . .' he pondered, 'the brain is like a gigantic hive . . . it *hums!* It hums the music of the spheres! Oh!' Angus Sphery blinked back his tears, and having pulled on his nose, thrust both his hands deep in his pockets, which rattled with trilobites.

'The Grail is not a cup of Christ's blood,' he continued, 'it is a cup of His Light. It is,' and Angus Sphery raised his voice to a high, shrill ringing, 'the *one* vowel God uttered when He cried: *Let there be light!* For in the beginning was the Word!'

'And she . . .' he mused, 'speaks a unique tongue, inspired, evidently, by divine intuition—for where could such an impoverished child pick up Chaldean? Zend? Patilavi? Parsi? I . . . I thought I caught something of *Old Chinese!*' he whispered with awe. Turning about he took his leave of them, muttering:

'I *must* return to her tent!' Away Angus Sphery stumbled, and his face was that of a man lost in an opium dream.

Chapter

9

The fever of language had claimed them all. That night Radulph Tubbs dreamed he stood before the pyramids of Kheops, Khephren, and Mycerinus. He saw them as they were meant to be seen, covered from top to bottom with hieroglyphs. In his dream he stared at the incomprehensible alphabet with a crushing sense of inadequacy. Yet as he looked the signs lifted themselves from the stone and like great pale birds soared into the air. Living signs they filled the sky. And Radulph could read. He read the soul of man; he saw the hands of God kneading beasts and men in clay and, blowing into their nostrils, imparting them with fire.

When he awoke the vision and the knowledge was spirited from him. Empty and enraged, he recalled only the feeling of helplessness which had submerged him at the onset of his dream. His answer to the darkness which contaminated and contained him was to seize Etheria from sleep and to take her with a savage force, nearly strangling her in the fury of a passion fueled by fear. The next day in her diary my sister wrote:

A HUNgry hole Eats at my heart

She was agitated, she could not be still; she moved about the house as a wind moves above the land, restlessly searching for a distant horizon where to settle and repose. She longed to flee and thought of nothing but escape. So sensitive did her hatred make her that she could no longer bear to breathe the air of England, tainted as it was by her husband's multitudinous industries. Tubbs's megalomania was such that by his fiftieth year he was called the King of Cotton, Paper, Glue and Bouillon Cubes, and a medal, freshly minted, was awarded him: Radulph Tubbs was made a Dragon of Industry. Queen Victoria drew the dragon herself.

Tubbs's new reign now extended to Egypt. The Civil War in America having deprived him of cheap cotton, Tubbs, in the fall of 1862, sent emissaries to Cairo to pressure Ismail, heir to the throne, into planting several thousand fedans—which Tubbs promised to buy. A large ginning establishment was projected also, and a rail to Zagazig; Tubbs was negotiating for cottonseed presses and a locomotive. And Baconfield's nephew, a genius perhaps, had sent Tubbs plans for a press to transform husks and shells and other residue into cattle cake.

I must also mention here that just prior to Etheria's vanishment, Tubbs was flirting with fertilizers and negotiating with the king of Egypt for one million ibis mummies. These he planned to grind into powder—a powder which he had first considered transforming into a profitable soup but the thing was impossible: the mummies contained too much tar. Though the broth had the colour of bouillon, it tasted like boiled pavement.

Wrapped in brittle bandages and encased in pottery cones, the mummies were stashed in catacombs at Sakkârah; Radulph awaited further plans from Baconfield's nephew for a crushing device to be constructed in Britain and shipped to Cairo. The atomized ibises, their granulated gum, shredded bandages, and pulverized crockery would be packaged in sacks, taken by camel to Alexandria, and shipped directly to Le Havre where a Monsieur Papan, *importeur*, was already scrutinizing Tubbs's terms. Radulph was on the verge of making his largest profits ever. The Egyptian king, longing for modernity and profoundly embarrassed by those subterranean Himalayas of throttled birds, was eager to negotiate.

The director of the Cairo Museum, Walter Bongo, protested, that is to say until he actually visited the site and personally confronted those innumerable drifts of incongruous bodies. He was appalled and ever after suffered a chronic despondency. As if to appease him (in fact the gesture aggravated the curator's precarious condition), the king of Egypt had one thousand of the dead things delivered to Bongo's home.

The man who replaced Walter Bongo had the objects shipped off to the Royal Museum at Copenhagen. In exchange, the Egyptians received a peat bog female in passable condition. The Danes, having no need for one thousand mummies, kept six and, having spread the rumour that the body cavities contained gold amulets, put them up for auction. They were snapped up by the bookish sons of the Danish aristocracy who, enlivened by aquavit and armed with razors, tore the birds to shreds.

All this goes to show that the world is a very small place, and what starts in Oxford may continue on to Copenhagen; that what has been buried as a god in Sakkârah may surface an abortive bouillon cube over two thousand years later.

CHAPTER
10

The garden volatilised as if by Satan, Etheria chose not to return to our father's house. Angus Sphery, blinded by his own aspirations, having sold his entire collection of butterflies and moths, had with a few precious trinkets coaxed the *Hungerkünstler* from her cage of glass and into Etheria's empty room. Those days I lived in acute misery, my poor head aching with the rantings of our brainsick mother and the *Hungerkünstler*'s hisses.

For a time the creature seemed content enough with a sole admirer who promised to make her famous and rich, and who had sold his rarest specimens to buy her dresses (all with silk slippers to match) and the glazed sugarplums she doted on and which were sent us from London. The creature, like any wasp, ate sugar and drank dew; her anorexia no sham, really, as those glazed fruits she sucked were, it is true, her only nourishment (and in her glass cage she had eaten *nothing*). I recall the monster (for as you shall see, that is precisely what she was) sitting in our best chair dressed in a vapour of lace edged in silver thorns, her sallow cheek swollen with a ruinous *bonbon glacé* as our father, Angus Sphery, unshaven and unkempt, his waistcoat spattered with ink, hangs on her every incomprehensible word. The *Hungerkünstler* had a genius for jibberish, *obscurum per obscuris*; one had to ventilate the room after her departure as there were so many hooks and horns of shattered consonants cluttering the air it was hazardous to breathe.

* * *

Throughout this period, Etheria, trapped in the New Age, dreamed of making herself lighter. She dreamed of air, of vanishing in thin air; she dreamed of evapourating. She dreamed of levitating, of growing wings, of transforming herself into a cobweb, an angel, a volatile gas. The more she dreamed of air, the lighter she became and the clearer did she perceive the irrelevant phantasmagoria which was her married life.

However Etheria was a realist. As she made herself lighter, as she cleared her head of the ill winds Radulph had set to blowing there, she recognised that she needed a purpose and a *métier*, she needed autonomy, she needed to secure an income. After a day's reflection one possibility presented itself. Rising from the floor where she had been stretched out surrounded by her jade army, she rang for the butler and when he appeared, expressed her desire to become a magician.

Thus my sister became the butler's pupil. He taught her everything he knew—which wasn't much; Feather had traveled with a circus as a child but before his master had given him little more than the rudiments of the craft, a plague of sorts had brought the circus to its knees and his master, as many others—including all the performing apes—had perished. Feather knew none of the Great Secrets, but he knew the principles of magic. He knew that the magician plays with the public's perceptions and memories; that he shows next to nothing and evokes all. And because he had himself manipulated his master's mirrors, Feather knew that mirrors were the lion's part of seeming.

He explained as well certain finger exercises to be practised daily with small spheres of brass, and tricks with knots, and how to pick locks with a key held between the teeth and hidden beneath the tongue. He knew the secret of one simple but effective deception upon which she was to construct her entire repertoire and which was the basis for her most extraordinary feats of prestidigitation. This trick was called 'The Hungry Coffin' and was performed with a pine coffin, six concealed mirrors, a length of rope, a piece of black cloth, and a candle.

As workmen scrambled upon the clock-tower roof or installed steam machines in the Palace to Industry and Infancy; as Angus Sphery carried Dr. Johnson to London and the last of the Nepalese horned beetles,

Etheria perfected the finger exercises and plotted her first vanishing act.

'My master,' Feather told Etheria, 'showed the crowd their own immense gullibility in the guise of wands and pentacles and cups. My master,' he continued, 'would bid his public gaze into the empty recesses of a tricked box as he, at his leisure, pulled pellets from his sleeves, and—much as a boy drops coppers in a pig-bank—larded a secret compartment to the back of his box. Then he would close the lid, shake the box furiously, open it and shower the stage with an entire tropical jungle's supply of collapsible, yet very lifelike snakes.

'Men like Radulph Tubbs,' said Feather, 'who believe only in what can be seen, or touched, or eaten, are not the exception but the rule. Whereas the things that truly matter cannot be carried about in the pocket and fingered.'

All this conspired to make Etheria into the wizard she was to become, this and something more. When Etheria set about to do her act, she gave herself over to it utterly. She was so completely a part and particle of what she was doing that on stage she was a woman no longer but impalpable spirit. To use Dodgson's phrase, *all that remained of her was her smile and the illusion of a miracle.* You see: famished for space, Etheria became a master at creating its illusion.

My sister evaporated prior to what was to be our family's greatest humiliation, greater even than the stories circulating concerning our mother's addled wits. With much pomp and publicity, Angus Sphery delivered a paper before Oxford's learned Philological Society titled: 'The Cosmic Dialects, or the Roots of Adam's Tongue: Being a Rational Investigation of the Universal Language Spoken by an Inspired Medium: The Celebrated *Hungerkünstler* of Prague.'

Angus Sphery had ascertained that the *Hungerkünstler* incorporated '*all possible primitive phonemes in her repertoire; she whistles, whickers, nickers, snorts; she moos, twitters, honks and hoots; she growls, buzzes and snarls. She is simultaneously harmonious and cacophonous. Language here exists at its purest, primal roots. On the following pages you will find listed: vernacularisms in Cherokee, Nootka and Tulu; Gaelic puns; paradigms in Turko-Tartar; Tagalog idioms; Umbrian substantives; Cushtic and Mongolic nouns.*' To my perpetual dismay he concluded:

'*The* Hungerkünstler *holds our Golden Age in her mouth!*' For this our dear but deluded father, whose mind had not been the same ever since our mother lost hers, was banished from the Society which had been a second home, scorned and snubbed by the men who had been his colleagues of a lifetime, and retired from his professorship precipitously. What little money remained was soon frittered away in ribbons and bonbons for the dreadful *Hungerkünstler*, who clamoured shrilly for a hat sewn of dead egrets she had seen on a fashion page, and a bed upholstered in velours and made to look exactly like a hollowed pumpkin.

When it became apparent that Etheria had run away (and she had taken *all* the jade with her: the very objects which had enslaved her she used to buy herself wings) Radulph Tubbs, in a fuming rage and desperate for clues, ransacked the house until he found one small triangle of scarlet silk which Feather had kept beneath his pillow—souvenir of Etheria and their own secret trysts. Radulph recognized it as the very piece Etheria had used to charm our mother, Margaret Sphery, not many months before.

The bow had been bent to its utmost tension. Swept away in a whirlwind of jealous hatred, Tubbs chased Feather through the house, past weeping maids and petrified footmen. Bellowing like a demon precipitated from the belly of Hell, he swore that he'd break the butler's bones and burn them to char in the furnace.

At last Tubbs cornered Feather faint with terror in the attic. The butler had no time nor breath to beg for his life. There in the dust, with his feet and his fists, Radulph beat his man into unconsciousness. Then kicking wide the window, he hurled Feather's bruised and helpless body to the freshly laid pavement below. May God have mercy on their souls.

Having long before purchased the silence of police and magistrates alike, Radulph was never brought to trial. The butler, an orphan, was buried in the pauper's lot on potter's lane and if the mysterious Mr. Marx left his calling card no more, flowers no less mysterious appeared beside the grave for many months thereafter.

From the day Etheria vanished, Radulph Tubbs swore revenge upon all

THE JADE CABINET 75

the Spherys, and all those whom Etheria had loved. His first act was to steal a manuscript from Dodgson's rooms. Fortunately, and unknown to Tubbs, its double had been delivered to the Deanery—a gift to little Alice Liddell. It is only now, years later, having read and re-read Radulph's memoirs and journals, that this riddle, among others, has been solved.

His next act was to seduce the spidery *Hungerkünstler* with gifts of candied chestnuts wrapped in gold leaf and Japanese dolls of porcelain, their oversize parts sculpted with precision. A vulgar, perverse nature devoted to the dubious pleasures of this world, and whose predilection for famishment found its roots in an unhealthy delight in dizzy spells and hallucinations, was easily seduced by hasheesh, the finest paste Tubbs procured for her via his business associates in Cairo.

The pumpkin bed was installed at the New Age and the plumbing, although I know for a fact that the *Hungerkünstler* never bathed. Her erotic voracity was such that Radulph was at all times too sated to beat her (in any case, this is how I imagine it was); he devoted his quieter hours to the fertilizer venture and placed a percentage of his profits in the hands of a detective agency—which bragged offices all over continental Europe—with the firm order that once found, Etheria be brought to him *bound*.

One final word before we move on—and the story now takes us to Egypt—in tracing the course of this narrative thus far, I notice that I mention chamber pots three times—a great many times for any narrative, especially one as brief as this! Times have changed and many of my readers will have plumbing and many, if they are North Americans, will have been *brought up with plumbing!*

But in those days we had the chamber pot and the pot had its own folklore, legends, and stories. True—I could remove it to its cabinet, shut the door and never mention it again. But no. The pot was there (a bold-faced reminder of mortality) and my readers sophisticated enough, I should hope, to have accepted their and mine own corporality.

For if, as with Etheria's prestidigitations, we were all of us but phantoms of air, it would be quite pointless for me to be writing this down, and Etheria's magic, God knows, could not have found an audience among fancies *in nubibus*.

CHAPTER

11

A bandoned by Etheria, who had vanished without leaving a trace, Radulph Tubbs attempted to salve his bruised dignity by projecting a trip to Egypt to oversee the removal of the ibis mummies, the installation of the great crushing machine, and the export of the dead gravel to France.

Baconfield, who was to be of the party, reassured Tubbs: the trip would erase Etheria's painful memory; they would live like pashas in beautiful tents of his own invention and take constitutional and archaeological walks upon *perfectly clean sands*: 'Imagine! No insects, no bacteria! No *seeds*, even! Just a fossil hugeness of lifeless sands beneath the ocean of the sky!' They would take the tents with them, and all manner of collapsible household items designed by Baconfield (the expedition and its expenses were much trumpeted in the daily papers).

The *Hungerkünstler* saw the trip as an excuse to expand a wardrobe which was, despite its wearer's diminutive size, Brobdingnagian; a creature of imagination, she ordered several *ensembles* of Nile green linen and a silk evening gown embroidered with asps, and sandals in the Egyptian mode. She dragged Tubbs to the Egyptian collection at the British Museum where he surrendered to his second hieroglyphic-induced crisis (his dream being the first); there *everything* he saw was crawling with asps—from inkpots to spoons.

Once the *Hungerkünstler* had finished her note-taking—she had brought Baconfield along so that he could make sketches for her seamstress and had twice lost her temper because his pointed nose was stuck in a *Champollion's Egyptian Grammar*, the pleated skirts on statuary interesting him but not at all—Tubbs, his head dangerously swarming with eyes and keys and lopped-off legs, herded them rudely out. He was generally irritable and tormented by shame. He was convinced that Etheria had run off with a lover because he could not imagine a woman capable of acting for reasons other than sentimental and without the complicity of a man. He supposed himself a cuckold with two great yellow horns rising from his skull for all to see. Surely this was when his odd affliction of the mind began: Radulph saw eyes everywhere glued to those phantom horns which—rooted deeply in his brain and fed by his palpitating heart—imbalanced his reason and sapped his forces. When Tubbs and the *Hungerkünstler* were not fornicating on swings suspended from the beams or in bathtubs filled with stout they fought together like wild beasts.

Baconfield was so taken up with the promise of the trip and the technical niceties of folding sinks that he did not much notice the storms that raged about the New Age; ever since the *Hungerkünstler* had taken up residence, it was as if a permanent swarm of cyclones pawed and raged and thudded around the house and in all its rooms. The *Hungerkünstler*, small as she was, had a voice to fill the world's largest opera house; when enraged, her screams were said to knock the birds dead from the trees and send the poor fish, belly up, to the surface of the Isis. The only way Radulph could stop her once she'd started screaming was to *la fourrer*, or that failing, shower her with presents: sugarplums and shoes, hairdressers and dentists (she was inordinately vain about her teeth, and, curiously just as Mr. Dodgson, was seen to by a dentist daily) and seamstresses, of which there were always two in her service. She kept them naked so that they could not secrete her rings in their pockets and so that, should they miss a stitch, whatever, she might prick their bodies, unhindered, with a pin. The creature's rage had something supranatural about it; surely anger was her way of getting back at Destiny which had kept her starving in the view of crowds for so many years. In passing, it is my personal conviction that humiliation leads to viciousness; the *Hungerkünstler* was incapable of tenderness simply because none was ever shown her; her anger was only as hot as her shame. Note, I do not excuse the nasty creature, but only attempt to understand her.

When one reads Tubbs's descriptions of his life with her, one cannot help but feel sorry for him, cad and assassin that he was. Their *ébats amoureux* were of such foul colouration as to endanger the sanity of the most hard-boiled *débauché*.

'She once boxed my ears so severely,' Tubbs writes, 'I heard bells for weeks. Another time she bit my tongue, necessitating three stitches. And yet, because of the state I was in, I needed her ferocity; her ferocity and her infinite capacity for depravity. . . . Although I admitted it to no one, not even to myself, I was ravaged by Etheria's departure; I was enraged. My violent confrontations with the waspish woman may have kept me from losing my head completely. When the *Hungerkünstler* bit my flesh, when she tore at my body with her teeth, when she slashed at my naked skin with her little cane, I, awash in the sea of my pain and my disgrace, suffered for Etheria less.'

These are the most moving pages in Tubbs's memoirs and I cannot help but be stirred by them; indeed, I have wept, even prayed for the soul of that infamous man! They are also, and despite himself, the most 'poetic':

'Anger and Humiliation, those pagan alphabets, could be read on our bodies, hers and mine, writ in a bloody script.'

After several months of saturnalia and several false trails (for weeks Tubbs's detectives had followed a tall, blonde, and taciturn lady's maid through fish stalls and into button shops) Tubbs, the *Hungerkünstler*, and Baconfield, accompanied by the Great Crushing Machine, set off by steamer to Alexandria and from there went up the Nile to Ghîzeh, where Tubbs, confronting them at last, was *appalled* (his own word) by the pyramids: *the death of Time and Space*. The victim of Baconfield's hobbyhorse dissertations on the pyramid as *shape of shapes* (and the reader, I promise, shall be illuminated shortly) Tubbs's imagination had transformed the ruins into an absolute, seamless geometry. Also, and as irrational as it surely was, Tubbs believed that the Sphynx, even though it has no eyes (having lost them, along with the nose, when Napoleon's mamelukes used it as a target for cannon practice) *watched his every move*; he was convinced that the great, maimed man-lion stared at those phantom horns, heavy as bronze, which Tubbs carried with him everywhere and which plagued him with migraines and fevers.

He was also plagued by problems relating to the installation of the crushing machine: in the first place it took several weeks to discover the whereabouts of the rails that had been sent on ahead, rails which were needed to carry the contraption—it was monstrously heavy—to shore. Once on land it had to be guarded continuously because its size and shape aroused much curious speculation among dragomen and *fellâhîn* who came from miles around to see it. Its purpose was kept a secret. Baconfield feared, and rightly so, that had the Egyptians, by nature superstitious, learned that sacred mummies were to be metamorphosed by those great hammers and cogs into fertilizer, they would surely have attempted to harm it. As it was, the thing's monstrous size and appearance had everyone convinced of its magical properties, so that it had not been on Egyptian soil an hour before a number of levers had vanished (and which may be seen, even today, hanging from the necks of infants suffering from eye disease, or plagued with pustular sores). The glass casings of the voltmeter and the barograph volatilised, as did a bascule, numerous screws and pulleys, a flywheel, a hexagonal button, and one small, strangely shaped peg which proved exceedingly difficult to replace.

Thus far the entire Egyptian adventure had so aggravated Tubbs's temper that Baconfield fled into the wastelands of those infinite graveyards whenever he possibly could.

If Tubbs hated Egypt, Baconfield, from the instant he set foot in that country, was seized by a nervous exaltation that contaminated him to the end of his days.

Ever since childhood, when his tutor had introduced him to geometry, Baconfield had dreamed of a perfect world based on the sphere, the cube, and the pyramid. He was the inventor of an ideal alphabet contingent upon the circle, the triangle and the square—an example of which I offer you in the shape of Baconfield's calling card (unlike any other I have ever seen):

Upon the back was laid out the plan for Baconfield's Ideal City-State:

a. Polis of Culture
b. Polis of Health and Education
c. Polis of Residency
d. Defenses
e. Moat

f. Industrial Embracement
g. Public Gardens
h. Arable Land
i. Duck Ponds
j. Quicksand

Whenever it was pointed out to Baconfield that if his city was impenetrable, it was also impossible for its citizens to leave it, Baconfield replied that this was the whole point: the citizens—having all they needed at hand, would not want to leave. Thus they would be no threat to environing territories (ideally: other such self-contained city-states). If all the world's cities were constructed on such a model, territorial wars would vanish from the face of the earth. And what existed beyond the city's rectangular boundaries? Forests teeming with ferocious beasts and those barbarous men who had managed somehow to flee, to survive the musket fire of the guards, the moats filled with crocodiles, the fathomless quicksands. In other words: *chaos*. Baconfield was a dualist and here his vision was contained upon a piece of cardboard small enough to be carried about in the vest pocket. A rectangle containing all that civilisation has to offer: opera houses, libraries, factories, duck ponds, hothouse peaches, prisons and watchtowers too. In other words: *culture*. And beyond: darkness pressing in on all sides.

'Imagine,' Baconfield liked to say, 'the world is a sea of ink upon which are floating blazing rectangles of pure light: the light of reason, sobriety, and punctuality.'

Here is an image of the ideal world as Baconfield explained it to Tubbs on the steamer to Ghîzeh:

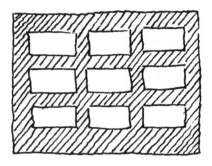

In another project, an entire country was contained within one tower modeled after the sacred architecture of Assyria whose temples, unlike those of Babylon, were reached by circumambulant ramps rather than by stairs (which, as we know, Baconfield abhorred, having tumbled as a toddler and badly bruised his noggin).

The beauty of this particular plan (if it can be called that; *beauty* was Baconfield's term) was that the wind washing down from the sky would sweep around the tower with a constant, invigorating whisper. Rainwater contained in a reservoir at the summit and made to flow down channels would irrigate the entire city. Graced with a profusion of suspended gardens, the ziggurat would resemble an inside-out cornucopia.

Having reached the base of the burgeoning ziggurat, the water would cascade into a great, circular moat that would, once again, isolate the city at its base. Pumps installed in the interior of the structure would send the water back up again to the top *et ainsi de suite* . . . (Baconfield also imagined a maze of earth, coal, and fine sand that would filter the tower's sewage before sending it—by way of subterranean canals—to the sea).

But as soon as Prosper Baconfield set foot in Ghîzeh, the ziggurat and the rectangular city-states were usurped by the pyramid to such a degree it is a wonder his skull did not change shape to fit the idea which occupied it so entirely. What did Baconfield perceive in Ghîzeh? He saw 'the virtues of integrity end to end. Indissoluble Absoluteness.'

Now he imagined a country contained within a vast tetrahedron of stone, secure from invasion, plagues, and weather. He spent three days and sleepless nights scheming a system of portholes and rotating mirrors to illuminate the entire structure within, a system of lifts based upon pulleys and weights. He wrote down his List of Exclusions: *There will be no birds within the structure, nor insects to soil it with their excrement, nor rodents, cats or dogs* . . .

Thus Baconfield, who had devoted his youth to dreams of a green Assyrian tower open to the wind, now gave himself over to the idea of City as Sepulchre. But the Sphynx's stare was killing Radulph Tubbs, and as soon as he had managed to gather together provisions, servants, donkeys, and camels for a trek to Sakkârah, the party moved on. Among the rubble and potsherds, mazes of dead birds stretching out in all directions beneath their feet, they set up housekeeping for the winter. Just outside the tents, workers scuttled back and forth with mummies held to their backs like outsize grains of weeviled rice.

Webbed in green the *Hungerkünstler* settled down to a life spent sprawled on carpets, tormenting servants and nibbling local sweetmeats: loukoum, halvah, and pistachios. Crushed by the heat and mortification, Tubbs sat in the shadows—every tomb opening was an eye fixed upon those imagined horns. He was pouring over the manuscript he had stolen from Dodgson's Oxford rooms:

Down, down down. Would the fall never come to an end?

Back in Ghîzeh, a railway one kilometre long had been laid and the machine moved to the mastaba of a sublimated nobleman of the nineteenth dynasty. Only the smokestack of the apparatus was visible, rising from the sand like the black stub of a colossal cigar. The machine had digested such quantities of dead birds that a fog of particulated tar saturated the entire region, and a vexatious grease adhered to the linen suits of the tourists who languished on the veranda of the Mena House Hotel a stone's throw from the Sphynx.

CHAPTER
12

Sakkârah is punctuated by one large pyramid; it is Egypt's oldest, and the tomb of Zoser the First. Designed by Imhotep, its curiosity is assured by the fact that it is made of five steps. A primitive structure, therefore, not unlike those Babylonian towers which inspired it. Baconfield looked at it with ambivalence, his admiration saddled by his allergy to stairs.

Because he was stuck there (Tubbs, barely functional during the day, insomniac at night, counted on Baconfield to divert him in the evenings), the architect, having viewed Zoser's tomb from all sides and having sketched it, filling in its crenations with imaginary bricks (so that it was transformed into a tetrahedron and a testimonial to his own onesidedness), began to explore, first the blebs and blisters of that infundibular terrain, and then, naked as a worm and carrying a torch, the very catacombs themselves.

The German scholar Lepsius had, but twenty years before, published a sketch of a section of the site, and a map had been made during Napoleon's campaign. Tubbs had procured both. But the maze of mummies stretched out for countless miles in all directions far beyond the confines of these maps, and Baconfield's excitement redoubled with each passing day. The sight of innumerable cadavers sealed within clay cones shaped like the wishing caps of wizards or dunces cast a spell upon his brain. Naked and panting, he explored on his ten toes the curiously cluttered galleries where the hot air was thin and the dust many centuries old.

Here and there a vertical shaft had collapsed filling an entire wing with tons of sand. Backtracking, Baconfield would find a new embouchure leading to yet another maze of passages. A man inspired, he knew not yet by what, he stumbled on and on for hours, for days and weeks like a gnat ever more entangled in a web, tirelessly exploring that lugubrious colander truffled on all sides with dead birds and knotted in shadows.

Sometime in late January the inevitable occurred: Baconfield's torch lacked fuel and he was hopelessly lost among the mummies. For a day and a night and another day, he dragged himself in the utter darkness among those hideously persistent cornets, ravenous for food and above all for water. As he told it, just at the moment when he had abandoned all hope he saw a luminous diamond shining in the inky darkness. Day was breaking. Baconfield had come to a fissure in the rock and sand that entombed him. Digging with his bare fingers through fragments of blue faience and bone, he lost his grip and tumbled down a shallow well. The well opened onto a partially collapsed chamber cluttered with a muddle of outsize alabaster vases which in the light of dawn glowed eerily. Erroneously he took the vases for eggs and feared he'd stumbled upon the nest of some colossal ibis.

For another hour, Baconfield battled with the vases until with terrible effort he managed to pull himself up and out to lie gasping and spent beneath the sky. He had come to the base of a small pyramid which, having lost its top, was in truth a queerly shaped cube.

The shock of finding himself saved just when he was certain to die precipitated a vision: Baconfield saw in his mind's eye a crystal pyramid which stood upon its very opposite: an inverted pyramid of air. On the threshold of exhaustion and inflamed by his sudden illumination, he burst into tears. He believed he had seen the world's consummate architectural and symbolic construction: a geometrical solid that contained its own negation. It came to him in a flash that:

Pythagoras was wrong. The universe was not made of intersecting circles but of pyramids; Fialin de Persigny was wrong: the pyramids were not dams destined to contain the shifting desert sands, nor were they, as some believed, silos to assure against famine, nor the magical concretisation of the sun's rays. Nay: they were the metaphysical building blocks God had used when He set himself the task of constructing this Universe.

Prosper Baconfield shuddered, recalling that the very mound upon which he and the pyramid sat symbolised the mountain which had emerged from chaos when Atoum created the world. This knowledge further justified his intuition.

Parched, bruised, spent, Baconfield fell back and closed his eyes. In his head he set to constructing a vast quantity of paper pyramids based upon the sacred triangle: 3, 4, 5. Six of these, drawn together at their points, made for a perfect cube. Perhaps he could have decided there and then that the universe was made of such handy blocks, but the cube seemed a dead thing, so he stacked six pyramids to the cube's six sides. The result was a polyhedron with twelve diamond-shaped facets.

In passionate concentration, placing two pyramids upon each diamond, he saw, incandescent in his head, a fiery Greek cross. It took him totally by surprise. This cross was the mystical confirmation of his theory. His mind swarming, Baconfield stacked on more pyramids and made a second cube—upon which he further assembled pyramids. By midday a mammoth, faceted sphere was set spinning in his head and he was raving:

'The towers of Assyria . . . *cones* . . . why they collapsed! The spiral . . . *a primitive form* . . . snails . . . other such refuse . . . the brute labyrinths of worms!'

He was discovered later that afternoon. Three *fellâhîn* carried him by the hands and feet back to his tent. Before he succumbed to sleep (and he slept for three days, waking only to sip sweetened water) he managed to whisper to Tubbs, and with utter conviction:

'My pyramids have sphered a cube!' a phrase for which he would be remembered, if only for a little while.

February proved an especially fruitful time for Baconfield. Rolled up in a rug, consuming vast quantities of thick, black coffee, stimulated by the *Hungerkünstler*'s unannounced appearances in harem pantaloons and little else, he eagerly demonstrated to Tubbs that all points are in fact not *round* as Pythagoras believed but *square* (i.e., the shape at the pyramid's base). He amused Tubbs and his savage pet by telling them that Angus Sphery was deluded: the primal language was not *verbal*, but, to all objective evidence, *geometrical and silent: the concrete language of crystals.*

It was in March that Baconfield gave Tubbs and the *Hungerkünstler* a telescope of his own manufacture in which the sun and the moon and all the stars appeared 'as they truly are': Greek crosses.

'In other words, there are no spheres nor circles anywhere,' he told them; 'the sphere is an illusion; the world is flat; the circle is nothing but a straight line joined end to end.'

The argument was tidy; Tubbs approved it. Yet it seemed that when he gazed out upon the cingulum of sand which had become his home, objects such as a camel had a way of *vanishing over the edge*. Tubbs was a man of money, not of science; he admitted to his ignorance and yet—did this not imply the spherical nature of the world?

'An optical illusion,' said Baconfield, 'explained away by the eye's own globulosity. What my telescope does is *cube the eye* and so set things straight.' Yet if the horizon, as seen through Baconfield's telescope, appeared very flat indeed, camels continued to vanish beyond it with exasperating regularity. However, Tubbs was so tormented by the *Hungerkünstler*'s antics with dragomen in broad daylight and so distracted by the yelps and screams of the servant girls she tortured that he could never keep his mind on anything for long and so the problem of the world's angularity ceased to plague him.

Baconfield's March madness brings me back to Dodgson. 'Let's suppose . . . ,' the dear man used to say. Well then, let's suppose that the mind is like a galaxy which, as it spreads across space, rotates. Within, solar systems spin, and sometimes something special happens—a meteor shower, the birth of a star, an eclipse. . . .

Let's suppose memories are like those special things; each star, each rain of meteors, each eclipse is like the last and yet it isn't because the mind, you see, *is never in the same place twice*. Like stars and eclipses, memories are simultaneously a rule and an exception.

Another example: Let's suppose the memory is like a jade cabinet, but a cabinet belonging to an infinitely irresolute collector. Each time we look inside, the jade appears to be the same, yet the mind is forever replacing one chimera for another that resembles it. Let's suppose the memory is a cabinet of chameleons and the mind as unstable as the moon.

Excuse my digression, but as I write all this down, it occurs to me that there are as many ways to tell a story as there are ways to remember it.

If I wish to describe Baconfield, do I start with the shape of his skull or his obsession with geometry? At this instant I recall his baby-fine hair the colour of sand which he would lose before reaching forty. Baconfield brings to mind a freshly hatched duckling, wet behind the ears, and duck-footed too. He was also something of a goose. But Baconfield's ornithological aspect might not be the right place to start if I want to give the architect weight. Yet, if his practise was a weighty one, he was himself very light, not much more than an agitation of the air (and now even less: a broken thread of souvenirs, a melody barely retained).

One more attempt: Baconfield was needle-thin. He had a funny bump on one ear like a little pink bead, and a long, pointed nose. His obsession made him tireless. He was simultaneously embarrassed and quickened by the *Hungerkünstler*'s erotic poses. Or, so I suppose. For now I am trespassing Tubbs's territory again and not my own. I only saw Prosper Baconfield twice; I was not there, with the three of them, in Egypt.

CHAPTER
13

When I think of the *Hungerkünstler*, I cannot help but think of Angus Sphery's study, that magical place where, as little girls, Etheria and I spent so many happy hours. I cannot help but recall with bitterness how, in order to appease the *Hungerkünstler*'s appetites (and so her temper) our father sold all those precious artefacts that had so deeply informed our hearts and our imaginations. First the beetles went, then the penguin eggs, next the albino mole, then Dr. Johnson (Father sold him to a French collector who also bought the Nigerian crocodile); he sold the butterflies to buy the *Hungerkünstler* one dozen pairs of shoes, the Small Blues and Painted Ladies, the Great Peacock Moths and the Small Angel shades. . . . He sold his stuffed tanagers, his lyrebird, his Quetzal; sold his six hawkbill tortoise shells, the pearl in the shape of a pig, the skull of a wistiti. . . . He sold everything, even the bottle of honey that had been procured from a hive built upon Thomas More's tomb, and the beautiful egg of a dodo. ('What,' Dodgson had mused with wistfulness upon making its acquaintance, 'is emptier than the egg of a dodo?')

But what is hardest to tell, and what shows above all else the piteous colouration our father's mind had taken: *he sold the jade:* the cane pommel once the pride of his youth; the cicada from Tubbs's cabinet and the chimera too; sold the earrings he had given to our mother, Margaret Sphery, to celebrate Etheria's birth!

I tell all this so that you will appreciate the power the *Hungerkünstler* wielded over men; her nefarious influence. When she left our father's house for the New Age, its redundant footmen, bell-pulls, and puddings, nothing remained in our father's study but a few fossilized clams and a coconut. Even the books were gone. Had his own devastation been less terrible, I know I should have hated Angus Sphery; as it was I could not. He was a ruined man, abandoned by the world. Having stung him to the quick and strung him up, the *Hungerkünstler* had sucked him dry. That winter he died a husk.

Alone I cared for our mother who did little else but stare at taches on floor and ceiling. She seemed to have grasped that her husband had perished for she carried articles of his clothing about, knotted to the hems of her petticoats, or stuffed down the front of her dress. And if by nature forgiving, as I write this—I freely admit it—I am consumed with hatred for Tubbs and the *Hungerkünstler* for the manner in which they annihilated my family and squandered its treasures.

In Egypt the *Hungerkünstler* grew fat. She sat in the centre of her camel hair tent surrounded by dishes of honey and whey, devising methods to torment Tubbs—including the attempted seduction of Baconfield whose whole being, as we have seen, was taken up elsewhere. Both Radulph and the *Hungerkünstler* became weightier: she in body and he in mind. Tubbs darkened also: it was as if his centre had somehow imploded; he absorbed light. In fact, he was as plagued by my sister's absence as by the souvenir of the sound Feather's body had made when it struck the pavement. That absence, that sound, were the very air that scorched his lungs, the terrible gravity that kept him earthbound. In his memoir Tubbs writes that in Egypt his sorrow *contained him as a cage*—as did his flesh. His flesh seemed an alien substance and yet it ruled him. He loathed the *Hungerkünstler*, yet perpetually desired her. She led him by the horns, those same horns which in his dreams had been transformed into the double crown of Egypt and which burdened him like a dunce's cap of solid lead. In a recurrent dream that plagued him throughout the month of March, Tubbs wore that dreadful crown and nothing else and the *Hungerkünstler*, a bloated, red spider, straddled his neck so tightly with her eight legs that he was barely able to breathe. Whipping him mercilessly with her cane, she precipitated him into a foaming maw of quicksand.

Tubbs always awoke screaming from this dream which he blamed on Baconfield, who had filled his mind with visions of tombs like gutted encyclopaedias submerged in sand. And more than once Baconfield had wagged that all the kings of Egypt had been horned by the greed of thieves and the stealth of time. How unsafe the pharaoh's sarcophagal house! How treacherous a man's vanity. Egypt was nothing more than one vast, pillaged jade cabinet!

'The Land of the Nile is a pudding,' Tubbs writes in his memoir, 'truffled with the grisly artefacts of human pride, heaving with mummies tarred and bound, and yawning with funerary chambers. B O U N D L E S S   P A G A N I S M! The mythical imagination is inescapable in Egypt, all pervasive: everywhere one turns one sees kings with the heads of lions, queens with the faces of crocodiles, hippopotamuses wearing dresses. Every article—obelisk, throne, and sphynx—is but a garish furniture which clutters death's antechamber.... And everywhere pyramids pustulating like the blebs on a plague-ridden beggar!'

It is a pity Tubbs was not an Egyptologist enamoured of the kings or even an enlightened collector, for he had an uncanny gift and could not walk two feet without kicking up an outsized alabaster thumb, a tauricornous amulet, a gold needle, an unnameable something-or-other black with tar (the matted viscera of a princess, the paw of a sacred cat), or the wee clay figure of a king defaced by sorcery or neglect. The entire country, as far as Tubbs could see, was one heaving cemetery hideously jumbled by the dance of time. He often felt the whole world listing, tilting, and on sleepless nights imagined that not only was the world as flat as Baconfield argued, it was a dustbin filled to the brim with trash. Which explains his firm resolve to grind to a fine powder whatever he could, mummies and tumble-down temples alike, an attitude mirrored by the *Hungerkünstler*. I explain:

The *Hungerkünstler* alarmed Baconfield (who was skittish among women to start with); more than once he had witnessed the fits of servants whom she had crazed with her incessant screeching and slaps. Inconvenienced by her hot advances, having oft, he hoped, with tact rejected her, and in an attempt to mollify her, Baconfield gave her a green peridot scarab of uncommon size and exquisite workmanship, which had dwelt in the chest cavity of a priestess for three thousand years and which he had bought from a *fellâh* in rags. The *Hungerkünstler*, who feared death and believed in magic, gave it to a servant who, before her eyes, reduced the precious thing to dust and fed it to her dissolved in wine sweetened with honey. So convinced was the *Hungerkünstler* of the amulet's uncanny powers that she pressed Baconfield for others. As it turned out the *fellâh* lived in a hovel which straddled a tomb; it sufficed that he lift a stone from a hole in the floor to enter into the mastaba of a corpse which swarmed with priceless scarabs of opal, peridot, *fayrûz*, onyx, and coraline. Some had the faces of rams, others of bulls, others had human faces. All of these were swallowed and digested by the *Hungerkünstler*. When a colossal *scarabaeus sacer* was uncovered by Baconfield himself as he rooted under his pyramid, he had it carried by four men to the *Hungerkünstler*'s tent. Rather than eat it, she turned it over to Tubbs who had ordered a second machine from Baconfield's nephew, very much larger and more powerful than the first, its purpose to crush the limestone temples which littered the environ landscape. Tubbs, who hated disorder (and so created it where'er he went), had all the temples he could seize—their columns in the lovely shapes of exotic plants, their carved friezes of undulating maidens—dismantled and transformed into chalk which was sent by barge downriver to the port of Boulak and sold to the masons of Cairo.

Thus as a plague of locusts did Tubbs and his party descend upon Egypt. Had Tubbs a pudding-pan large enough, he should have steamed the whole country with currants and eaten it up with a runcible spoon.

Fleeing the steamy triangle of which he was, by no fault of his own, the third party, Baconfield now spent all his time digging beneath his pyramid in an attempt to find its antithesis. On the third day he found a cadaver, the feet of which had fallen off. The leg bones poked out from the blackened flesh like stilts. Had he been less exhilarated and less driven, perhaps he would have seen in those pollarded remains a sign and a warning.

Before Baconfield had the thing removed, Tubbs came by to see it; thieves had cut into the cadaver's bandages centuries before to grab piteously ineffectual charms; in rifled rags the body lay revealed: desiccated, bituminous, hideous. In anguish Tubbs reeled away violently retching.

Tireless, Baconfield continued to mole and burrow. The hole he had left beneath the pyramid was very deep indeed; for some obscure reason the cadaver's feet appeared after another ten days of constant excavation.

'Things flow about here so!' Tubbs agreed with Baconfield when the architect surfaced at dusk caked with salt and sand. 'We will be leaving soon...'

These days Tubbs's voice had a way of fading; he no longer finished his sentences. 'The ibis mummies are nearly all removed and...' The party would be leaving for Bubastis to exploit a cat's graveyard. Pressed for time, illuminated by his vision, Prosper Baconfield returned to his digs that very night.

Sometime in the middle of March, Baconfield, as he scrabbled after his phantom vision, had a second illumination. He saw—as clearly as if it had been penned in black ink on white paper—a plan for the first house that ever was: the house that Adam had built for Eve in the garden of Eden. This house was, in truth, a tetrahedron of cunningly woven branches and it stood within a rectangular yard which—although he did not realize this—replicated the sketch he had made many years before of the ideal city-state and enlivened the backside of his calling card.

Just before the final entry in Baconfield's notebook, there is a sketch of a truncated pyramid flanked on all sides by deep orbital trenches, a vast vascular cellar gaping beneath, and a tunnel worming into it from north to south intercepted by a second tunnel from east to west.

On March 31st, just as the last ten thousand ibises were being removed from their vaults, Tubbs heard a stifled noise and felt a small wind: Baconfield's pyramid had collapsed into the faithful absence Baconfield had provided beneath it.

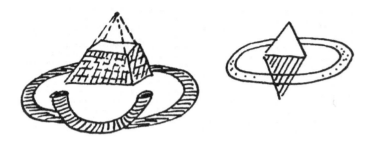

Sketches from Baconfield's notebook.
It is apparent that he was also looking for a fossil moat.

On the first of April, Radulph Tubbs received a letter from the Arab astronomer Mahmoud-pacha-El-Falaki, who had uncovered a number of ram mummies at Elephantine and was writing to enquire if Tubbs was interested in their purchase. If the astronomer knew that Tubbs was a buyer of mummies, it was evident he did not know for what purpose. 'The mummies are well preserved,' he wrote, 'especially the horns which are in excellent condition.' He went on to say that the visit to Elephantine had given him the idea to restore the *Nilomètre*, a dilapidated column which the Egyptians used to measure the yearly flooding of the Nile.

Tubbs was convinced the letter was a hoax. Those rams's horns, implied tusks, and even the damaged column, vexed him deeply.

CHAPTER
14

In his memoir Tubbs writes:
    'Despondent in Sakkârah after Baconfield's dreadful accident, I turned once again to the stolen manuscript: *Alice's Adventures Underground*, with the mad hope it might give me clues to things which had until then evaded me: Etheria's reasons for abandoning me, the invisible knots which tied her to Dodgson and never to me and which had made her his friend and not mine. The tale's meaning, if indeed it had any, was persistently elusive. As far as I could see it was a story devoid of sense. And yet it was a profoundly subversive text, giving, as it did, *reason to a child*. When I read, for the last time: "Away went Alice like the wind," I could not help but writhe as a man flayed alive, for I read: Away went *Etheria* like the wind. The manuscript's heroine ran after a white rabbit; I could not know it then, but Etheria had also *run after magic. . .'*

    Reaching a resolution at last, Tubbs left his tent and made his way across the sands to a secluded spot scattered with the rubble of a pagan temple which had once, or so it seemed, been inscribed from top to bottom with serpents, knots and knives. Radulph set Dodgson's manuscript on fire and watched with hunger as it was metamorphosed to ashes. He thought the sight would give him satisfaction and the act liberate him: it did not. Instead it deepened his despair. His old rival's manuscript had been—he realised it now—the one artefact that linked him to his vanished wife. More resonant by far, far more potent, even, than the white silk stocking he secreted in a deep pocket in a piece of luggage which, in a fit of jealous rage, the *Hungerkünstler* had discovered and torn to shreds with her many pointed teeth.

'The loss was not great. All that scrap of cloth had ever done was to recall the violence of our encounters—the bruises I had left on flesh so pale it recalled fine ivory or cream—and to fill me with remorse. Beside the memory of Etheria's infinite delicacy, the silk appeared weighty and rough, it weighed upon my hands as a mail of lead. I wondered at the violence of my passion, the extent of my loss, and reaching out into evening, clawed at the very air as if to grasp the woman I had forever lost.'

When the last page of Dodgson's manuscript collapsed into ashes, Radulph suffered an acute sensation of desolation. A small breeze stirred and lifted the friable bits of charred paper. With his gaze he followed one minute flake which, taken up into the air, rose in a spiral so perfect it might have entranced Baconfield. Just when it disappeared a wind announced itself with a low whine and turning, Tubbs saw a tower of sand perhaps fifty metres away, gyrating like a jinnee released from a bottle. Mesmerized, he watched as this apparition tore silently past. The phenomenon lasted but an instant; the phantom tower spun away to the east and in the dusk dissolved. Night descended and a red moon wheeled up from the horizon. The bloody orb brought to mind the gaping mouth of furnaces and all at once Tubbs longed for England, the sight of one thousand chimneys vomiting smoke into the sky. As he returned to the great tent which groaned and creaked like a sailing ship in the wind, he thought it no sane dwelling for a civilised man:

'I wondered that I had lived like a bedouin all winter. That I had taken up with a woman who lacerated my flesh with her nails as if I were a mere coachman. Yet I know I had done so only because my senses had been invaded by a species of poisonous fog ever since Etheria's absence.

'Firm in my resolve, I changed my linen, pulled on my boots, and confronted the *Hungerkünstler* with my resolution: I would return to England *alone*; I would see to her immediate expenses *and no more*. I suggested that if she preferred not to return to the ignominy of the fairground (which would demand strenuous self-denial lest she wished to be billed not as a Hunger Artist but as Fat Lady) then she, who was capable of little else than screaming, biting, and pricking, and making the lives of her protectors into Hell, should offer herself to the first sheikh into whom she might stumble; sheikh wanting—the first horse-butcher.

'The *Hungerkünstler*'s tent reverberated with her screaks; she tried every trick she knew to shatter my resolve. Unable to bear the sight of her any longer, I bade my servants—all aroused by the bedlam—to guard my tent, and my ears filled with wax, went to sleep. When I awoke the next morning the sand all about was furrowed by her kicking and her flailing. She had rent her hair and clothes and sat upon my threshold, penitent and bruised.

'"You look a mess," I told her. "No sane horse-butcher will want you." Her wailing ignited the day but I was off to Cairo and so abandoned her to servants who, I would not be surprised, paid her back for all the violences she had inflicted upon them in the past, who sheared her of everything including the purse I had tossed, as I left, at her heart. Strangely it was only after I had thrown her out that I fully realised how much and for how long I had held her in horror. . . .'

To have rid himself of the *Hungerkünstler* had not freed Tubbs as he supposed it would, but only deepened a conviction of futility. The day prior to his departure for Cairo he had stopped to luncheon with a pasha of his acquaintance: Tewfik Pasha's cattle had all been struck down by a plague and it seemed all the world was littered with smoking corpses. After lunch Tubbs accepted a pipe that tasted strange; to his dismay he was informed it had been filled, as indeed was customary, with the powdered dung of a hippopotamus. Crossing those blasted lands he hoped for the last time, the sight of all that sand truffled with mummy further depressed him. Astride a donkey that had been whipped into a murderous frenzy by the running footman who followed Tubbs everywhere brandishing his *kourbash* and howling, he was certain to have caught a glimpse of a human jaw with all its teeth clenched upon a fragment of archaeological linen.

Until the last, Tubbs never did succumb to the collector's instinct. Would it have been possible to pave that entire country over, concealing its morbid history beneath a thick shell of armatured cement, he should have had it done.

He no longer dreamed of planting pyramids in England to the glory of industry, but only of the comforts of the New Age, its plumbing, plum puddings, and umbrageous rooms. But as his ship would not sail for a fortnight he would have to make do with the Horus Hotel and perhaps a little boy to wash his feet and soothe his mood. Yet as he rode he entertained this fantasy: that Etheria would be in Cairo waiting for him, was even now inspiriting his rooms.

CHAPTER
15

His rooms at the Horus were empty. Flanked by threatening bronzes by Barbedienne of Paris, Tubbs sat down at a desk the size of a bull's sarcophagus to write his detective agency in London a letter both plaintive and enraged:

Sirs.

I am paying you, and famously, to solve a tangible affair, in other words: a *worldly* matter. My wife, Sirs, is not spirit *but flesh*; she exists in space and time; her feet touch the ground when she walks (for never, in all our months together, did I once see her *levitate*). *My wife does not float through the air.* Therefore, *she has left traces.* Why have you still not found them?

My wife is a woman, Sirs, not an angel, not a bird, nor is she a dream moment of the mind. Surely she has not volatilised. My wife is no gas, Sirs, nor is she vapour.

Sirs: Despite the fact that I am acutely aware that sense has long been dethroned by dullness and perspicacity by blindness, still your incapacities startle and amaze me. I can only conclude that if you masquerade as detectives, you are in point of fact nothing other than whimsical muddlers.

He knew his disappointment was ridiculous, that Etheria, wherever she was, could not know that he had taken rooms in Cairo, and that had she known, she would not have come. And yet he had expected to see her there. As he entered the vast marble lobby cluttered with boxed banana trees and statuary and forbidding onyx mantelpieces, he found himself gazing eagerly about, startled by the ringing of his own blood in his ears. When he did not see her, his desolation was complete.

That night he could not sleep. Embraced by melancholy, it occurred to him that delight had been offered him but once and that he had badly fumbled. Something precious had been given him, something precious which he had broken. And now, having lost her, he was banished forever to the land of opacity. Haunted by feelings he could not fathom, he was the prisoner of gravity.

At dawn, after a night of profound unrest, Tubbs went down to the hotel gardens. Servants sprung everywhere from the shadows but he waved them away. He wanted to do something he had never done: to walk alone in a garden, and at dawn.

The garden was a luxurious place, a thicket of bananas, daturas, oleanders, and acacias surrounded by date palms. Paths were bordered by rose bushes and in the centre played a large alabaster fountain. In sadness Tubbs walked and as in the first air of day the leaves all about him stirred, he was startled to feel the tangible presence of Etheria. The sudden proximity of the woman he loved was of such potency that he stumbled; his servant who had been trailing him silently reached out and held Tubbs fast. That embrace, so unexpected, brought tears to his eyes. And then Tubbs was sobbing. To his profound embarrassment, despair had mastered him utterly. Clinging to the boy, he made his way back to his rooms where he remained the prisoner of fever for several weeks.

Throughout this period, Radulph thought that he had never felt heavier, weightier, and yet, paradoxically, he had never felt more insubstantial; even his own servants' corporeality took him by surprise. It was as if—even when he trod the thick silk carpets of his rooms in the soft leather slippers which had been made to his own specifications and which were so comfortable he might have been walking on air—he continued to tread upon the refuse of graves.

When he had gathered enough strength to look back at the years during which he had waited for Etheria and wooed her (or rather, wooed our father Angus Sphery), it was as if he recalled a limbo-land, as if he had wooed but shades and won but shadows. Indeed the world appeared to him as inhabited by phantoms, and he a phantom too.

Tubbs did not know it, but he had fallen in love. Etheria's memory ruled him with an imperious constancy which rendered him helpless and enslaved. Slavery was a celebration of his passion, but because the object of his cult had vanished, and by his own fault, love's celebration was affliction.

He knew he had denied ecstasy. He had been brutal and selfish. He had used Etheria, worse: he had attempted to break her. And there had been no profit in it, only loss. The fabulous wealth he continued to accumulate as if magically (that month a flood had destroyed the greater part of his rivals' cotton) he received as a mockery.

He craved Etheria and he hated her. The very idea of her absorbed all that was potent with possibility within him, his capacity for cognisance and clarity. I imagine that he must have also reviled himself but did not know it. He had not yet begun the painful enquiry into his own heart.

Overnight his years burdened him. For the first time he thought that very soon he would be an old man.

Curiously, there were brief moments when her memory caused rapture and the thought of her elated him. Then, for the brief instant of a sigh, he believed that the world and his own energies were boundless, that he was not a half-man horned and dim but a prince on the very verge of a great adventure: *He would find her.* He would beg forgiveness. She would see at once that he had changed, how her loss had transformed him utterly, that he was charming now, that he could entertain her brilliantly with riddles and stories as inventive as Dodgson's. He would offer her feasts, delicate gifts, voyages, palaces; his wealth was hers, for her pleasure. They would live a life of inspired passion in an Eden of his own construction (with a sinking stomach he recalled Baconfield at this instant). He imagined telling her, as he caressed her hair, soft as the silk of milkweed, that every time a Tubbs mill factory whistle blew it was for her and for her alone, that on both banks of the Nile cotton was being harvested for her pleasure, that Baconfield's (poor Baconfield!) nephew's machine chugged on ceaselessly so that she, Etheria, his beautiful wife, would have the life of her most fantastic dreams.

But just as this vision took wing, it collapsed at his feet in a heap.

Etheria's face was replaced by smoke and confusion and he found himself worrying about cotton worms, the rising cost of spindles, a chimney in Lancashire about to collapse, adultery and death.

If a moment before his face was diffused with delight, now it took on a purple hue, paled, darkened again, turned almost black. And he, who had stood tall and radiant and still, visibly thickened and lowering his head, and bowing his shoulders, set to scowling and pacing his gloaming chambers again. Surely he was not sane, but possessed by tumultuous weather. The burning enigmas of love had degenerated into chaos and I like to think that he who never prayed supplicated our Lord God to pull the baggage from his back and lead him out from the universal haze of things and let him wander in the world again with an unencumbered heart.

Tubbs's servant, a small, dark boy of twelve, regarded his master's variegated moods from a corner of the floor. As still as any ebony gazelle, he sat in the restful shadows and when summoned bathed his master from a large copper basin, or pressed fruit upon him, or, with a palm-leaf fan created a soothing breeze. But when at last Radulph's spirits had chilled to inertia and he refused to leave his bed, Camel knew enough to fetch a doctor. He found Dr. Spritzner in the lobby. Spritzner barreled into the room, a clear speaker, robust and triumphant. He pulled the curtains aside, threw all the windows open and purged the room of its welter and Tubbs of his chaotic flux of incertitudes. Next Herr Spritzner ordered breakfast, and coaxing Tubbs to table, embraced him in the gossip of the city as, with a flourish, he delivered to his plate a tiny toasted quail.

Spritzner was irresistible and even as he gnawed a bone, Tubbs was talking. His servant Camel, grinning and scraping with delight, was sent running to an outfitter's for a leather travel case the Herr Doktor had described as just what Tubbs needed for the trip home. (Both men discovered to their astonishment and delight that they had booked passage on the very same ship.) The travel case was made of hippopotamus and Tubbs, feeling very much better, joked he'd rather keep his brushes in it than smoke it. Then off to the *harâra* and its cleansing hot steam. There Radulph and his new friend perspired together and had their joints cracked satisfactorily. After a vigorous lathering, rinsing and toweling, the two sat down for more coffee and Tubbs, who desperately wanted to talk but could not bring himself to talk of *her*, told this wonderful man whose open face and attitudes had so quickly brought him back to life about the profound disgust Egypt had wrought upon him and the Hell which had been his keeping house with the *Hungerkünstler*.

'Vat you neet,' the doctor prescribed, slapping Tubbs fraternally on the back, 'Vat you neet iz to forgotting zis *Giftmädchen!* Vat you neet iz vimmen! Nize, ztout vimmen!'

That evening Spritzner took Tubbs to the Café Khamâsîn, where the orchestra was female. The music they played was Viennese. Sipping date brandy, Radulph could not help but notice how the breasts of a lady flügelhornist trembled whenever she blew into her instrument. With joy he discovered that his spirits were on the rise. Throwing back his shoulders, Tubbs boasted to the doctor about profits he had made on the local market by pressing cottonseed and husks into cow cakes.

But that night, in the bed of the instrumentalist whose lungs had so thickened his blood, Tubbs was bound by incapacity. He wanted the woman badly but those imagined horns had returned to haunt him; they weighed him down and weakened him. At the moment of penetration he was undone by the thought that he was himself about to be entered by the tusk of an elephant, the horn of a rhinoceros, or a great, green finger of jade.

Sirs.

Incapacitated by distance, in constant struggle with demoralisation, I can only hope that your lumbering team has at last swung into a precipitous fury, inspirited and confident to the last degree. Soon I sail to London and with the highest expectations! I do not wish to be met with vain excuses and lame explanations!

Gentlemen: Noah's dove found a place to rest its feet; my wife has feet and somewhere, *somewhere* she is resting. My wife is no dove, Sirs; no creature of cloud! But flesh and bone! And so must leave *substantial* evidence after her wherever she wanders. I am paying you to gather clues, not rents in infinity. . . . To find a perfume, a pattern, a *person*. And this person is *my wife*.

FIND HER!

CHAPTER
16

Simultaneous with Tubbs's defeat, and just as a larval worm which, when its time has come to fly, breaks through the dry crust of the earth to crawl beneath the sun and spread its wings, Baconfield, further crazed, surfaced. His beard and hair were knotted with lumps of tar, and fragments of shattered crockery had penetrated his skin. He appeared in the middle of the night in a forsaken, nameless oasis somewhere in the region of Bibig, raving about the dangers of hollow places and the need to fill them in. The *fellâh* who found him dressed his festering wounds, gave him datura tea to drink and led him to a hut which, because it attracted scorpions, had been abandoned many years before. Just as Adam's, the hut was made of mud and it exuded a smell peculiar to places favoured by arachnids. Baconfield sighed and slept.

The next day, and the next and the next, Baconfield scrawled odd patterns in the dust with his toes, for his fingers were occupied by the vermin that riddled his beard, the flies orbiting his mane, the chipped bowl of *fûl* set steaming before him three times a day. Before he dipped his fingers into the *fûl* he scrutinised its vapour and noted variations in the way it dodged the dust motes of the air. Although nobody knew it, and his expressionless face implied otherwise, Baconfield was gripped in the contemplation of the limited world into which he had so recently resurged. Evenings, when the sky darkened to red cooling the atmosphere, and mornings when the air at his feet was aroused by the heat of the sun, the crazed architect, sitting in his bower of flies, considered

the possibility that the air is a fluid comprised of spirals. He intuited a
constancy in the disorder of the air and in the ebb and flow of village
life: the braying of donkeys, the moaning of camels, the clouds of bats
and mosquitoes that every night engulfed a minaret of mud, the shrill
games of restless children and squabbling of wives, the migrations of
the vermin that infested his own face, the random patterns of the flat
beans and congealing butter in his bowl, the scuttlings of scorpions in
the cracks and shadows of his walls, the frequencies and intonations of
the cries of pigeons flocking together in their square towers or circling
the tiny hamlet and its Brobdingnagian palms which, at this season, were
laden with dates as smooth and as yellow as amber beads:

> *croo, crōōō !*
> *croo, crōōō !*

Baconfield listened to the pigeons and at the same time contemplated the hesitant, veiled dances of the tattered clouds which appeared,
tenuis umbra!, for the time of a sigh overhead in the deep blue sky of
Egypt. Being still, he noted that the rhythm of his own heart was far
more erratic than he had ever suspected, that like the humming of the
ubiquitous flies his heart was subject to sudden fits and starts. And upon
the clay walls of his hovel he marked with a thumbnail in code all the
information which he harvested during the day (and, because he rarely
slept, at night).

For example, if one had read Baconfield's walls in the winter of
1864, one would have seen that throughout the month of November,
the Heavens dropped 734 stars.

The small community of *fellâhîn* looked after the tall, beaked
Englishman because they knew he was mad and therefore holy. (And
did not Plato himself assert that madness is superior to a sane mind,
for the one is only human, but the other divine? Indeed, Baconfield was
often seized by a mystical hilarity. . . .) Soon they were bringing him their
own bowls of *fûl* because it was apparent that therein, having surrendered
to the eyeless eye, he could see the imminent events that made their
lives unique and terrible and precious: marriages and conceptions and
treachery; flood and fortune and death.

The inspired fog that had claimed Baconfield's brain would dissolve enough for him to comply, if enigmatically, to the questions put before him. Sometimes, as he looked into those greasy pools, he thought, however briefly, of the ideal alphabets of his own youth and of Angus Sphery's quest for the tongue of Adam. Beans, after all, were alphabets as good as any. And sometimes, as he gazed at those falling stars, or felt the breezes of evening play catlike about his crusted ankles, he recalled Etheria and with a pang—perhaps all that was left him of conscience— wished he had, when in the world, allied himself differently.

For he was no longer of the world, but, since the mishap with the pyramid, his brutal burial and providential resurrection, graced with innocence, ruled by intuition, and living in a limbo-land of the mind far from wanton dealings. Bodiless. Had his brain been kept ticking in a jar of sugared water his state would not have been altered except that he might have been grateful to be unshackled of the trouble and bother of parasites, thirst, heat, and hunger.

His Arabic was serviceable if limited, and so Baconfield could utter, and with conviction, his parched voice and Oxford accent exotic enough to keep his neighbours on the breathless edge of mystery, the words that encompassed the future:

> *shuft* . . . (I have seen)
> *ba 'deh bukra* . . . (the day after tomorrow)
> *ishâl* . . . (diarrhoea)

Even when on days of impenetrable introspection Baconfield was reverently prodded with a stick only to utter such incomprehensible phrases as 'a better macassar oil' or 'boil it in ink,' he was nevertheless cherished as the living evidence of divine intervention by people who, until his coming, had been, or so it seemed, forgotten by God.

So would Prosper Baconfield's life have continued if it had not been interrupted by the appearance of the *Hungerkünstler* straddling a flea-ridden ass. She had been traveling for countless days in zigzags and aimless circles all alone—every single one of her ill-treated servants having abandoned her. Parched and in furious temper, she found herself surrounded one late afternoon by a squawking crowd of ragged *fellâhîn*. Because she was so obviously European—she wore a palm-leaf hat, carried a tattered white parasol, and, although she did not know it, the glimmering cotton cloth she had chosen many months before at the Cairo bazaar and had made into the dress she wore was the cloth traditionally used for the wrapping of corpses—her ass's bridle was seized, its rump slapped—she, at a pace she was not accustomed to, led to a dust bowl fringed with palms and to her amazement delivered up to Baconfield.

He did not appear to recognise her. Baconfield was lost in thought: a pattern had emerged in the tumultuous canopy of flies that followed him wherever he went, a pattern, or so it seemed in his intuition's most luminous recess, strikingly similar to that of the bats which invaded the evening, the perambulations of the wind. . . .

Barking for water which was delivered to her in buckets from the nearest well, the *Hungerkünstler*, having deeply drunk and refreshed her face, seized Baconfield by the ear and with her habitual violence and fistfuls of sand, scrubbed him clean. Later she bid a number of small boys to build a fire of green eucalyptus branches in the centre of the architect's hovel to scatter the scorpions which, falling to the dust with small, dry thuds, their bristling tails erect, were smashed to bits by the swarms of children who had come running from all corners as soon as the word was out that a red-eyed woman was giving their oracle a bath and fumigating his house.

The *fellâhîn*, startled at first by the sight of their sage being man-handled by a monstrously fat woman dressed like a corpse, soon took the event as a pretext for festivity. As some children ran off to fetch the fresh coura-stalk bedding for which the *Hungerkünstler* had managed to haggle (she promised her badly battered parasol and half-dead ass in exchange, and what else was she to do? Where else was she to go? Tubbs had left her enraged, humiliated, and broke) others ran to fetch the *âlâtîyeh*. They came scurrying with cautious celerity—for most were blind—with their bells and tambourines, their fish-skin drums winking with tortoiseshell, their bells and flutes of scored and stippled reed, their sheep-gut zithers and violins made of coconuts. They played their tuneless songs, 'so exasperating to the European ear' (quoth Tubbs), repetitive and, or so I've read, obscene; indeed, a man dressed only in a loincloth and a leather belt strung with a skirt of beads and intoxicated on barley-bread *boozeh* danced in a disgracefully provocative manner to the cries of 'Aah! *Allâh!*' Waterpipes were shared, and sweet, thick coffee in cups no bigger than thimbles. Very late an *awâlin* sang a song which she invented for the occasion and which made everyone laugh:

> O ye angels and devils who witness the world
> from below and above on high,
> have ye seen how a sage
> has been tamed by a shrew?
> How a blessed fool
> has been screwed?

which he had. For just at the moment Baconfield had come to perceive the divine formulae that dictate, in darkness, the world's apparent randomness, just when the thumbmarks on his walls comprised an exhilarating pansophy and he stood poised on the verge of omniscience, an uncircumscribable chaos had swept into his life.

CHAPTER
17

The *Hungerkünstler* (whom Angus Sphery and Radulph Tubbs had habituated to luxury) made it clear that bowls of *fûl* were no longer sufficient salary for the sage's predictions. Sitting on a clean mat in her scrubbed corpse's clothes, her white mane bound up in thick, twisted strings of camel's hair, she haggled over prices. She still spoke in tongues, which was baffling, also terrifying. But her intention was clear and within a week the *fellâhîn* were bringing clay vessels running over with black honey, the buffalo cow's first milk after calving sweetened with sugar cane, a young turkey roasted to a turn. Some brought her the little noseless figures which had once, in the afterworld, performed a dead king's tasks. Prices fluctuated with her moods. Inflation set in and so precious things began to appear in little bundles at her feet: a blue-paste baboon, a silver drinking cup.

Baconfield was no longer able to sit in quiet contemplation of the world. When he was not reading the future, he was sweeping out their pesthole under the *Hungerkünstler*'s directions, or carrying washing to the waters edge, or stirring beans upon the fire—beans which, more often than not, were enlivened by a piece of meat. For she had been discovered by a roaming dealer who was willing to buy all the artefacts she had. He paid her miserably, but such was the *fellâhîn*'s dependence upon Baconfield's predictions that the *Hungerkünstler* was, little by little, accumulating a not negligible nest egg.

Her power over Baconfield was exhaustive. Whenever she caught his eyes wandering, or that peculiar expression of ecstasy which overspread his face whenever the bells of intuition were ringing in the depths of his mind, she would shout some new order at him or, if need be, even slap his face. Her constant insults, which banished what little was left of his self-respect, included: *beetlehead, lackwit,* and *witling.* Baconfield, having succumbed to a species of selfless innocence ever since his second and dramatic accident (the first being, as you will recall without rehearsal, the time he fell on his head as a babe), allowed himself to be manhandled and bullied by the unstable creature for whom he had become: sweeper, char, hairdresser, laundress, and dragoman.

And the *Hungerkünstler* cured Baconfield of a most curious habit. He had fallen so low as to examine, with an attention altogether morbid, his own excretions, convinced that in chamber lye and *egestae* lay certain keys to the mysteries. Yet I suppose I can see his point: if, as Angus Sphery insisted, all aspects of the material world reflect the creator's face, a pisspot should be as good a place as any to strike illumination.

While we are on this subject, so distasteful to most—I once read that the turds of the Grand Lama of Tibet are dried according to sacred rites and kept lovingly in little bags of embroidered silk, or white paper, or fioles of silver, or amber, or other precious stuff. This Holy Merde functions as amulet. (According to Tubbs's memoirs, the Bedu of Egypt bake their bread upon fires of camel dung and apparently to no ill effect as these are a handsome people, slender, *spirituel,* and gay.)

This digression upon the Grand Lama's Holy Merde makes me think that Baconfield was on to something; after all, as Mr. Darwin has so brilliantly shown recently, mutability (for which digestion is an apt metaphor) is at the heart of all things. If the Lord is anyone, He is Proteus. God is everywhere—of this my life of reflection and abstinence has convinced me. And if I were a famished Bedu, eager for my daily bread, I imagine I might in time of need see grace, nay, see His face in the turd of a camel.

This is just one of the many overwhelming paradoxes that animate my life.

Back to Baconfield. Despite slavery, his predictions remained uncannily precise, as if that space in his head and that space alone remained inviolable. And when, on a clear, silent evening he saw in his mind's eye the arrival of a burning cone of sand one mile high, he, by shouting to the air from the dark certainty that animated him, was able to warn the village of impending disaster and thus not only save them, but assure for himself a place of honour among them forever.

Two memories only kept Baconfield moored, tenuously it is true, to this world. Without them the *Hungerkünstler* would certainly have rendered the architect irreversibly idiotic. Because of them, something vital, dim as it was, held fast.

The first memory was that of a view he had seen many, many months before as he had stood upon the barren plateau beyond Bedrashen—of all Egypt's pyramids in conclave: Sakkârah stood before him, and to the left Dashûr, and to the right Abusir, and far away Ghîzeh. In the rosy light of dawn the pyramids glowed like ripened apricots and peaches. Indeed, those beloved pentahedrons were received by Baconfield as a vision of infinite grace, the fruits of the gods set out for his own delectation upon vast saucers of violet shadow. It occurred to him that something holy had been offered him that morning. And this vision, even under the *Hungerkünstler*'s despotic reign, continued to nurture and sustain him.

The second memory, curiously, was of my sister, whom he had seen but once, but whose presence at the table he recalled with a shudder when, upon an evening he had, with such shortsightedness, accepted to pave a dream garden with granite slabs. Even now Baconfield was haunted by my sister's eyes, the eyes of a child who has been unjustly and severely punished not because she has committed a fault, but because the ways of the world are cruel, inscrutable, and unjust, and the power of adults boundless and blind.

If life in that gigantic dustbin had taught him anything it was this: the gardens of the world are sacred spaces.

Other than these two memories Baconfield's mind was an arid country, the mirror of those pharaonic lakes which evaporated centuries ago, the melancholy mound of a ransacked grave picked over by the wind.

The months passed. The *Hungerkünstler* had taken to roaming the countryside with a small band of thieves. She had uncanny luck with tombs, could, with no maps to guide her, read the incomprehensible landscape opacified by time and into which she had plummeted, witlessly, like a chunk of extraterrestrial matter. Had Radulph Tubbs such luck with tombs it is probable that he—who could not help but kick up teeth preserved in gobs of aromatic gum or brittle bones penetrated to the core with bitumen and which creaked beneath his boots like tubes of glass—would have uncovered only the four canopic jars containing, respectively, the large intestines, small intestines, heart, and liver.

If she continued to hunger for sweets, having expanded to proportions altogether mythical, wheezing as she walked (for no ass was broad enough to carry her), her greed for wealth was far the greater. The pendulum of her sixth sense left to skew this way and that, had her spinning in the salt fields like a teetotum until, with a small, shrill yelp, she would point to a mound or hollow, so like all the others, before collapsing with a thud among her voluminous shrouds. There she would sit, beneath a new parasol, fanned by two or three Nubians, as her rabble of thieves dug a deep hole in the evening.

Need I say her gift of clairvoyance was fatal to archeology in that region, but as she was very clever, no one suspected her until it was too late. Spectacular objects began to surface throughout the world; collectors from Denmark, Germany, Sweden, America, France, wherever, knew that if they contacted a certain Kâmel Nâsîr Zigada in the *muski*, they would be offered objects of unusual quality: crocodiles of pure gold, their tails set with scales of azure glaze, elaborate ivory powder boxes engraved with peacocks or pictures of lions and unicorns playing draughts, precious *ushabtiu* figures, the combs of an unknown princess, her red ivory jars of frankincense and eye paint, copper coffers, poison rings, diadems.

Thus in the free flow of amoral commerce, innumerable keys to the past dissolved away, as the *Hungerkünstler*, buffeted by famishment, her sails billowing with immeasurable greed, plotted her escape from Egypt.

On one occasion Kâmel Nâsîr Zigada had brought her from Alexandria a small silver pistol of deadly accuracy and beauty. In the cool hours of the early morning as Baconfield mended her hems, she stood beneath the date palms firing into quantities of large unbaked storage jars of yellow clay. She liked to joke to Zigada that the jars brought to mind her former lover's adiposity. By spring a heap of fractured crockery was the proof of her lethal commitment. She was now a 'crack shot' and, firm in her resolve, prepared to track down her former lover and deliver a bullet to his heart's centre.

CHAPTER
18

Tubbs's voyage across the Mediterranean and the Atlantic was uneventful if ill-tempered. The salt air eroded his sinuses; indeed, such was his mood that everything deranged him.

As it turned out, Herr Doktor Spritzner's dynamic personality, so beneficial on land, proved a burden at sea. Tubbs, unhorsed by his failure with the flügelhornist, resented the German his successive shipboard conquests and the strident vulgarity of his *propos*. By numerous similes, metaphors, and other contrivances of speech, Spritzner painted unwearably racy pictures of his amorous nights.

One morning, Spritzner, misconstruing Tubbs's ill humour, explained with a wag ill-fitted to Tubbs's impatience that his consuming interest in the vagaries and variabilities of the female anatomy had little to do with lechery and owed much to the physician's interest in physiognomy. Their friendship ended dramatically when just as a radiant redhead entered the dining room, Spritzner, his mouth full of toast, sputtered in Tubbs's ear:

'See dat vun? She haf a *porple* pussy!'

The cold, sobbing wind of sexual failure raged through the mazes of Tubbs's mind. He threw down his fork, scattering omelette, and abandoned the table. Spritzner ran after him:

'But *vye*? I haf ovended you! My friend! *Mein ami!* Not to be running avay so vast!'

He grabbed Tubbs by the shoulder.

'You—you unspeakable Turk!' Tubbs spat, squirming in his grasp and bristling like a hedgehog cornered by hounds. 'You disgust me! Take your low pieces of business elsewhere!'

Ever after, when accidentally the two met (which happened often although they did their very best to elude one another) the German, civil despite his anger, bowed. Averting his eyes, Tubbs held his breath until the dreadful moment had passed.

Without Spritzner's influence, the oppressive weather at anchor in Radulph's skull worsened so that by the time he reached London, the torpor of Cairo had evolved into a mighty squall. As wired as any dervish, Tubbs took a fast hansom to Babbitt, Abbott & Cobb, Detectives to inform himself of what he already knew. If they had 'turned over every leaf' (Cobb), 'sifted the air for clues' (Abbott), 'searched High Heaven' (Babbitt)—the mystery of Etheria's vanishment remained intact.

Radulph erupted. He slapped Babbitt with such force that he dislodged several teeth and he threw him from his chair. He swept many months of paperwork to the floor and trampled it and drenched it in ink. He sent Abbott's freshly stewed pot of tea tumbling onto his lap and emptied his new tin of gingernuts into the ashbin. He overturned the ashbin onto Abbott's desk. He threw every book he could seize against the walls and nearly strangled Cobb with his own cravat. Then, bellowing gall, Tubbs stormed out the door and into the arms of a pieman whose hot pastries flew into the air before tumbling into the street, causing Cobb, brandishing a cane and screaming, to slip and fall and break a leg. (Later, when billed, Tubbs refused to pay damages. Instead he hired a lawyer, for it had occurred to him that by abandoning him, his wife had committed a criminal act.)

The train was scheduled to leave for Oxford within the hour; still breathless, Radulph bought his ticket and installed himself in the plush interior, taking care to pull the blinds and to wrap his legs up in a rug, although the day was unseasonably hot. Within moments he was sleeping soundly and did not awaken until the train was well underway and a fragment of exasperating nonsense was entering his dream:

'*What sort of insects do you rejoice in, where you come from?*'

Tubbs awoke to see that he was no longer alone but in the company of a little girl and her governess; the governess was reading to the child from a little red book. When she saw that Tubbs was awake, the woman nodded and smiled agreeably; the child, however, put her fist to her lips to suppress a laugh—Radulph had been sleeping with his mouth open. Irritably he shut it and thought: *I grow old.*

Again he slept and his dreams were strangely animated by the curious profusions the red book provided; he half-awoke once to wonder if those oddities expressed some sacred thing lost to him. He thought: *old and without a wife.*

Oxford is a city as changeable as the moon. With winter it eclipses, sombres into dotage, but in late spring youth rules the streets, and jocularity, and the pretty fables of amorous adventure. Oxford is beautiful in June: the air is golden, birds orbit the spires, and butterflies animate the alleys.

This sweetness was lost on Tubbs whose house—shadowing forth as a mammoth from the bogs of time—dwarfed the sun and entombed his mood. And as the shadow of Baconfield's clock tower, the tallest in the city, lay adderlike upon the streets, Tubbs expanded. No more satisfied with cloth and cow cake and fertilizer, he acquired new holdings: a lead mine, a paper mill, three foundries. The wind of Tubbs's anger was blowing; he wanted nothing more than to see the smokestacks of his impotence scorching the sky; he wanted to see the colour of his rage written everywhere upon the air. I believe that Tubbs had actually declared war upon the air.

My special intention is to tell things as they were, as best I can. And yet, and I admit it freely, hindrances abound. There is so much I do not know or do not recall and so must imagine. Also, as I set about to unfold my subject, I must deal with Tubbs's vanity, lies, and transient moods—for his memoirs are stained with anger, guilt, remorse, passion, pomposity—and even humility. Just like the Devil weaving nets: *he wishes to convince me.* And sometimes he does.

Then again, I must be vigilant of my *own* weakness; a virgin, I cannot help but be shocked by some of the more intimate details of the *mémoires* and, to be perfectly honest, at times they do make me wistful although I am myself particularly unphysical (and believe that the physical is an inlet for evil). Having never *known* man I cannot help but be moved by these passionate avowals even if, on the other hand, I can never lose sight of their base (or bestial) nature. And Radulph was once a very handsome man; as I recall, Etheria herself once commented upon his profile and the breadth of his shoulders. His height, too, added to his attractiveness. Once when he came to luncheon, I remember thinking: the man carries himself like a king! But then he began to speak—of profits and bricklaying and all the ponderous furniture of industry—and in order to defend themselves, my thoughts, like my sister's, drifted off and away to other things.

Also, it occurs to me that an unhappy man is always a misreporter. Surely the same may be said for a woman. As a girl I admit to having on occasion luxuriated in thoughts of love, looking for meanings effectual in the eyes of strangers. But this is innocence, for the darker realities had been hidden from me. Yet they were on the edge of my consciousness (had not my father, Angus Sphery, collected the private parts of butter-flies?) and lapped at my dreams like a lake at the shore. I admit to a vague sentiment of sumptuousness which, despite their violence and vulgarity, Radulph's memoirs awaken. Even now the man is a mischief-maker! (Although when one considers how things turned out, I needn't justify myself.) Still—how can I admit to such feelings, knowing what I know? Thank Heaven I have Christ as my guide and inspiration, for although I am now over sixty, the abyss appears to have the very same attractions as when I was a lass of fourteen! To think that I have, and not so very long ago, dreamed of the hot breath of that murderer beside my cheek; I have actually dreamed of his hands. Then again, perhaps the explanation is mere loneliness? I must get out more. I live too much in the mind and this house boils with phantoms of all ages.

Not long before he died, Dodgson proposed a 'Doctrine of Mist': that things exist only because we perceive them (and we exist only because we are capable of perception!). It occurs to me now as I write that if *all is idea* then nowhere is the inherent contradiction of corpo-reality more evident than during the act of remembering.

Memory, I think, is an act of magic. In other words, we transform the outer world of facts: rabbits, hats, silk scarves, and painted trunks into those things we wish to keep, for whatever reason. And what I give to you is magic too: from out fragments of fur, I give you a living rabbit. I hold him by the ears. His eyes are pink, his nose is wet, he struggles—then lies limp with fear. You see him, yet he is not there: he is an illusion. Look: I drop him back into my hat and with a smart clap of thunder, the hat collapses into a thin, flat disc. A delicious aroma of baking fills the air.

I call a boy up from the audience and hand him the flattened hat. I ask: 'Boy—can you tell me what this is?' 'It's a meat pie, yer Honour!' (I forgot to tell you: I am disguised as a man.) 'Taste it, then!' I cry. 'Don't be shy! I can certify to its freshness and quality.' 'A rabbit pie!' he beams, gravy spilling down his chin. 'Clever lad!' I hand him a chocolate shilling and send him back to his seat.

I believe it was Sam Johnson (and this story justifies Angus Sphery's allergy) who, having asked one of his small sons to count some objects in the street, whipped the boy severely for claiming there were four when there were three. Had Dr. Johnson been my father, surely I would have been beaten too. For to make the present tale stand up and wag, oft must I take three for four and four for three. And more often than not, there are *no* objects to be seen because the fog of forgetting or unknowing is so thick I perceive but vague lumps floating in the stew.

Furthermore, even if I describe things exactly as they were, the language I use is not divine, but a poor imitation, a stew overcooked and lacking salt. Imagination is the only spice I have, and those muddling emotions that memories inspire—Radulph Tubbs's and my own. But I have nibbled around the edges of my subject too long.

CHAPTER
19

Sometime that autumn (and this was the autumn of his return from Egypt) Tubbs, who had been stewing in his own juices for months, set off with servant and coachman after his smokestacks. He writes: 'I took my pleasure in their unanimous tendency to spoil the proportions of any landscape.' October found him rattling through the dust-burdened roads of Kent where he paid a visit to Baconfield's nephew. The precocious pest had patented a pesticide. Tubbs proposed its manufacture.

On the way home, somewhere between Greenwich and Carlton, Tubbs's carriage confronted a seething wall of revelers—several hundred in all. Regardless of age or sex, each one was wearing horns: of cattle or goat or sheep or of gilded paper; some were made of tin. When the carriage was engulfed by this obstreperous mob, Tubbs fell prey to irrational panic. He was convinced that the world at large had received some news of Etheria, that the nature of her adultery was of such extraordinary tenor and her triumph over him so entire that his humiliation was known to everyone! In this quiet corner of rural England three towns at least had banded together with the sole intention to shame Victoria's Dragon of Industry! (Tubbs had recently received that prestigious title.)

Radulph bassooned to his coachman to ride on through but the crowd pressed too thickly; it was impossible to pass else plow British citizens underfoot. As his man pulled down the blinds, alien voices surged around them. Radulph hid his face in his hands and for the first time since babyhood, prayed, acknowledging with every atom of his being that Hell was not yet obliterated from the map of the universe.

The encompassing clamour (which included catcalls and trumpeting and whistles) appeared to last forever. Radulph's carriage was jostled and kicked, the very air thick with songs that aptly described his imagined condition. Yet it was over within minutes, leaving Radulph with chattering teeth. Had it all been a satanic vision? Was he losing his mind? His servant lifted the blinds; sun cascaded into the carriage; he was handed a bright silver tumbler of old port and with a sharp crack of the whip was off again to arrive, and on schedule, at Carlton.

There, as Tubbs stepped down from his carriage, a wench proffered him a piece of gingerbread from a tray she wore hanging from her neck. Famished, Tubbs claimed the cake before he saw that it had been cut to the shape of a cuckold. Howling, he thrust it from him and ordered his coachman to take up the reins and drive him home without once stopping. This he did, all the way to Oxford town, nearly killing the horse.

It has been said that the world conspires against sinners. Not long after, Tubbs, taking air, passed a bookseller's window and spied on display the very same little book he had glimpsed on the train upon his return from Cairo. Vaguely intrigued, he approached the window and was struck to see that the book's title was very like that of the manuscript he had destroyed at Sakkârah.

Radulph entered the shop and took up a copy; indeed the book was the same if longer and illustrated with caricatures: he had always hated caricatures. He bought up the entire stock and had it delivered to the New Age directly where it was used, all that night, and the next and the next, to feed the fire. But the matter proved hopeless. Tubbs's newly engaged agency, Willow, Pillow & Pond, informed him that the ubiquitous fairy tale was immensely popular, a favourite item in bookshops all over England, Ireland, and Wales. And they informed him of what he knew already: the author, Lewis Carroll, was his hated rival of long ago: Charles Dodgson, the 'foppish, effeminate stutterer.'

Just as Tubbs had taken the Saint Luke's Day Horn Fair as intended insult, so did he perceive Dodgson's *Alice*. His obsession with Etheria's loss, horns, and the Oxford lecturer of geometry became one. He paid his detectives to track Dodgson everywhere, which they did: to the seaside, the theatre, up- and downriver... Willow, to his infinite discomfort, sat in on Dodgson's lectures on mathematics.

When Radulph, aware of Dodgson's inclination to photograph little girls in the nude, wrote many letters to their mothers—who had given their permission assuming that Dodgson was as harmless as a maiden aunt, indeed more so, and far more beneficial to their daughters' minds, moods, and tempers—they discarded Tubbs's missives as the banter of a crank. When once at a dinner party Tubbs attempted to slander Dodgson by referring to him as 'that perverse posturer,' he found himself ostracized for the rest of the evening. Such is the potent witchery of my old friend's little book!

Baconfield's nephew visited Tubbs in January to discuss his latest invention: a metal-plated, steam-powered gun-carrier which, he said, would 'revolutionise war.' As they strolled together through the Palace to Infancy's icy landscape's locomotives, cotton gins, and elevators, Tubbs seriously considered the manufacture of such an object. Later, over port, it occurred to him that if an industrialist *really* wished to acquire a fortune, a fortune not in worldly but astronomical terms, he should *take on war:* governments have massive amounts of money to spend and war uses up massive amounts of material. The Queen—who had seen pictures of the machine—thought it 'very droll and pretty! A little like a toad on wheels.'

Baconfield's nephew's success with pesticides had him experimenting with the lethal powders also, with which to 'dust enemy encampments.' 'But who is the enemy?' Tubbs wanted to know. 'Everyone is a potential enemy,' Baconfield's nephew informed him. He told Tubbs: 'We are at the forefront of a new era.' Tubbs, suffering from angina and the onset of emphysema, and stuffing his face with Yorkshire pudding, nodded, breathing heavily in agreement.

Radulph had found much comfort in the meal and the young man's brilliant company. He proposed a legalised partnership. Their plans were real, robust; they imparted the transient world with a palpable gravity.

Their glasses empty, the two men decided to take in some entertainment.

They rode to the Metaphysic, where the evening's offerings included an Irish ballerina, a sword-swallower from Afghanistan, and a magician named Zephyra.

As the evening's first two acts progressed, Tubbs brooded: why had he allowed Baconfield's nephew to marshal him through slush-encumbered streets reeking of coal to see a spinster female spinning in her tutu like an ugly teetotum, an anorexic Arab ingurgitating cutlery, and—any moment now—a magician? Tubbs, who liked to sit on solid things, to roost upon the plaster eggs of reality, entertained an especial hatred for magic. When the sword-swallower clattered off to sparse applause, Tubbs braced himself expecting the worst.

CHAPTER
20

As the audience shifted impatiently in its seats, a stagehand shaded the gas lamps with screens of coloured glass, and the stage, saturated with blue light and losing all definition, was transformed into a nebulous somewhere, an immeasurable expanse of indigo air moted with fine particles of silver. Laboriously breathing, Radulph Tubbs was transported despite himself.

Somewhere—it seemed at the base of his spine—a bell rang and in that dreamy magnitude a shadow of sound lay suspended on the air; it caused the velvet curtains to ripple and dissolve. The sound thinned and thinned until only its ghost remained—an echo so eerie Radulph clutched the arms of his chair as if he feared to lose his balance and tumble into an abyss. Again the bell sounded. Just as a lump of white sugar melts in a cup of black coffee, Radulph felt himself dissolve.

With each sounding of the bell his mind wandered to Etheria. She inhabited him as if, particulated, she had entered his lungs and was traveling the mazes of his veins. When for a third time the bell rang, an enigmatic figure appeared at the centre of the stage. She was veiled, and in that oceanic light half visible.

Radulph held his breath. The instant he saw her his heart ignited, burning with a chilling flame. Indeed, Radulph shivered as the magician's hands revealed themselves, erupting incandescent in the airscape.

Slowly her hands orbited the air; gathering speed the calyxes of her sleeves extended, whipping the air like sails. A bird of night, she was sailing the air and as she sailed she gathered stars and planets up, plucked them from their zodiacs. Apparently she was juggling spheres of glass but *silently*: the only sound in the hushed theatre was the sound of her sleeves.

As the spheres looped and wheeled they also multiplied; each sphere released engendered three, six, twelve, eighteen—and Radulph could not tell if this was a mere trick of mirrored light which created a seemingly infinite set of phantoms, or if she concealed an infinity of spheres up her sleeves. Nay: the thing was impossible. The silk sleeves, so thin as to appear almost immaterial, contained only a pair of slender arms—arms which caused Radulph to gasp with famishment and fear, for he believed he saw the arms he'd lost, those arms which once, the morning of a fair, had enlaced him with a tender eagerness his own beastliness had murdered, an eagerness, the shy promise of a hunger, they might have shared.

Looking into the magician's eyes, Radulph saw those same eyes he had once seen burning in the face of a small child as she stood, damp and stained with grass, in her father's study. Eyes of a wildness untamed, a species of confusedness reflected there which had never clarified itself for him but which he had perceived at once to be a 'relishable quality.' A 'relishable quality' that proved his undoing, for in fact, her inchoateness had enraged him. He had wanted to reduce her to a quantifiable lump of reality he could paw at his leisure.

But now a magic lantern had been illuminated in the wings, several perhaps, and the spheres, or so it seemed, were diffracting the multiple images of fanciful animals. The air was roiling with dragons and phoenixes and unicorns and owls; turtles, tigers, a griffin, chimeras. His heart wildly thrashing, Radulph thought he recognized all the creatures of the jade cabinet. A sea of constellations swarming at the throat of night, they lay scattered, scurrying and volatilising across his field of vision—

As when he had found Etheria sleeping among the jade and had pressed himself upon her, awakening her; had felt her palpitating beneath him, the small, fearful animal of her fleeing his fire. He recalled her face, her limbs captured and bent to his will, her knees like smooth stones, her smell of lilac, the mossy garden of her, the picture pavements of her. He recalled how—when he had violated her with the jade phallus—she had cried out.

Cried out *silently*, a throttled bird, a star falling from an immeasurable height into the gullet of blackest space. He had taken her then, raged into her, and somewhere, deep within herself and despite herself, the glowing mud of her had answered: *yes*. Yes. He was certain of this! He who was blind, who had been damned with impercipience from birth, had, for an instant, *and because she had answered him*, seen the gardens of the world infused with divine breath, seen an alchemical forest the sight of which transformed the dead wood of him, the deaf, dumb, blind stump of him into a tree of life with limbs of sweetness, laden with fruit hanging heavy with infinite sweetness.

Zephyra the magician was bathed in an opal light, and she stood beside a screen encrusted with circular mirrors. Radulph saw those devastating eyes and hands reflected and proliferating as she continued to evoke volatile creatures from the air, surging, waxing, diminishing . . . and she was stepping back into the dissolving screen which filled a finite space at the centre of the stage. Slowly, with the slowness of clouds eclipsing the moon, *she was gone* and the stage empty. The theatre was saturated with a heady scent of freshly crushed roses; in an instant that too disappeared and Radulph found himself blinking at vacant air.

For several long moments he sat as if stricken by acute impotency, but then he scrambled to his feet bellowing: *Seize her! Seize her!* So great was his haste to reach the stage that he climbed over men and women still seated in their chairs.

Just as he had stumbled to the edge of the orchestra pit a man with ink-stained fists knocked him to the floor and began to batter Radulph's face in a rage so irresistible Baconfield's nephew needed the help of three others to tear him away. Through a veil of blood, Radulph recognized Cobb of Babbitt, Abbott & Cobb, Detectives. Standing with difficulty, Radulph screamed:

'*You donkey's arsehole! That magician was my wife!*'

Perhaps because my sister's performance had been so spectacular and the public so incensed by Radulph's violent eruption in the still instants which followed, the men who held Cobb did not hold him near firmly enough and the moment after Radulph had insulted him, Cobb broke away to give him a fearful kick in the jaw which nearly severed his head from his spine.

Foaming at the mouth, Radulph tumbled to the floor. Before losing consciousness he looked up at Cobb and then beyond him and into the crowd, where he saw, as sharp as a cutout of freshly painted tin, Dodgson standing with two little girls, each to an arm. Dodgson's shocked face appeared to expand and, leaving its body behind, to float up into the air. There it stayed, staring down upon Tubbs long after Dodgson had with urgency ushered the little girls away from the scene.

When a constable came to investigate after, Etheria—for it could only have been she—had already vanished. All that remained was a hand-tinted photographic slide which the constable stepped on unwittingly and crushed to a powder. Although she had done nothing, committed no crime other than that of enchantment, this time her vanishment intrigued the authorities. Zephyra ceased to perform. However, my own research into the matter uncovered several possible aliases: Nebula, Angelica, and above all Stratosphera, who performed at the Empyrean in London for sixteen weeks and whose act included a spectacular levitation. Indeed it was said that Stratosphera leapt into the air and *stayed there* as she juggled burning candles.

Radulph, wearing a neck brace, his face concealed in bandages, wintered in hospital and Cobb, carted off to Bedlam, was, poor soul, driven mad within weeks. They kept him trussed like a chicken and, to cool his temper, soaked him six times daily in ice water.

It was there that Cobb and Baconfield met.

CHAPTER
21

As Baconfield's nephew has but recently succumbed to his ultimate contrivance's shortcomings (a species of chamber to be flooded with gas, its intention mysterious), I do not know *how* Baconfield got to Bedlam, but I can imagine it: the *Hungerkünstler*, eager to disencumber herself, may have written to his nephew who may have sent for his uncle or, perhaps, even gone to Egypt to fetch him. Discovering just how batty his uncle had become, unaware of the exceptional quality of his preponderations, and being something of a rascal—Baconfield's nephew dumped Baconfield in the asylum.

As you may recall, after his Egyptian incident, Baconfield devoted himself to meditating upon the hidden structures of hazard and believed he saw an underlying order as exemplified in his bowl of *fûl*. The pyramid that fell on Baconfield's head had stamped out his dogmatism; I mean to say that ever after he wasted no friction in attempting *to impose his own order*. The architect had become a sage.

It occurred to Baconfield that just as he had himself been thrust from the raging abyss of his mother's womb into the world, so the shapely spheres that spin in timekeeping orbits were born of chaos. Like the stars, Baconfield was 'in and of the whirl of it!' a phrase he repeated tirelessly throughout his last years to Cobb, his doctors, myself—anyone who would listen.

To give his nephew credit, a quiet room in the quietest wing of the Hospital of Saint Mary of Bethlehem in London was paid for, as well as a special daily allowance of *fûl* cooked *al dente* the way Baconfield had come to like it, over a fire of dung and flavoured with a little red pepper. It was Baconfield's nephew who suggested that his uncle and Cobb be put together; he liked that symmetry: their destinies bespoke an inevitable confrontation. Both had, after all, an intimate connection with Radulph Tubbs. Above all: when Baconfield's nephew had placed his uncle in Bedlam and asked about the other patients there, Cobb's case was described to him in detail only because it was so very curious. The man was obsessed with turbulence.

'So is my uncle!' Baconfield's nephew had cried. 'We must introduce them to each other.'

In this way the two became chamberfellows; Cobb, always oddly agitated ever since his misadventure with the straitjacket, stood out in flagrant opposition to Baconfield's mysterious inertia, which, after all, was not mysterious to anyone who knew of Baconfield's obsession. Baconfield sat still as a stone simply because he had something to watch. In his mind he was mapping Cobb's critical navigations of the room: Cobb appeared to be paddling a birch canoe in whirlpools all the while pitching sticks at hounds.

If to the unenlightened it appeared that Baconfield was frittering away his time indulging in torpidities, he was in fact furthering his theory. It was becoming clear to him that what appeared to others as Cobb's vexatious automatisms were, in fact, a dance and *lyrical to the last degree*. Each bobble of the head, each tic afforded the best kind of suggestiveness, contained cargoes of meanings. Like the unvolitional atoms of the First Chaos, each flailing of the arms was an expression of circularities, routine fidelities—the expression of a mechanism complexly ordered in its malfunction. In other words: Cobb was subject to a blithesome, a beautiful, *a blessed* fury and the two men were swept up and away in a constellation of sympathies.

I have in my keeping (the result of much badgering) a voluminous set of papers that are covered with Baconfield's careful scrawls and which, I am convinced—once I am able to pull the mess together into a manageable shape—could be of great value to the world. I believe Baconfield was blessed with an intuition of paramount importance. I oft discussed the case with Mr. Dodgson, who eagerly shared my conviction: Cobb and Baconfield enjoyed an extraordinarily fruitful friendship in Bedlam.

CHAPTER

22

Throughout his recovery, Radulph thought obsessively of Dodgson. He oft dreamt of him and in these dreams saw him strolling with an agonizing slowness along the pebbled beaches of an alien sea, Etheria beside him; the scene in muted sepia and cream like *moving* photographs (one of Dodgson's many playful obsessions) (Tubbs did not dream in colour).

Later, when he was mobile, he, having dismissed his agency, alone tracked Dodgson, just as he had years before when Etheria was but a child. Night after night he stood on the lawns at Christ Church among the giant oaks staring up at my friend's darkened windows, or, when the gaslights were brightly burning, perceived him bent over a book and pacing, or hunched at his desk building little geometrical figures of cardboard and glue. Once Dodgson made an obelisk and Tubbs recalled with sadness how Baconfield had called obelisks 'pyramids with *very* slender bases.'

Except for this curiously eccentric behaviour with female children, Dodgson appeared to live a life miserably circumscribed by convention. In all the time Tubbs shadowed him, he did not once see him in the company of a female older than twelve. Radulph trailed Dodgson, wearing out pair after pair of shoes; and although he could not know it, the students made a joke of him: they called him the phantom walrus—an animal, it is true, Tubbs had come to resemble, swathed against the fog and mist in an oversized raincoat (Tubbs was losing weight), his *favoris* bristling on his cheeks like tusks and glistening with weather. I think it would be safe to say that throughout this period, Radulph was lost, having volunteered his liberty in exchange for the profound enslavement of a vile fixation. And if not so very long before he had spent his tormented nights in a furnished room in Cairo staring stupidly into the flame of a candle and dropping captured mosquitoes, bloated on his blood, into the flames, he now considered each past act of infamy in the light of a painfully won understanding: as he stood in the rain he questioned for the first time *just what sort of a man he was.*

It comes to me that, to give Radulph credit, his quest was precipitated by love and so, perhaps, was not so very unlike the Christian's quest for God. Tubbs was, after all, a sentimental man and motivated by passion, which is, I should think, a Christian instinct (or God should not have thus informed our hearts). However, I should not wish to labour this point for fear of indulging my own vanity. The path to God's kingdom is not given to everyone and in my darkest moments I cannot help but wonder if this—my own telling of the tale—is not of the same pernicious character as Radulph's foul shadowing of Dodgson.

Never had Radulph Tubbs spent so much time under and about trees; he took to noticing them. And the grass underfoot, and even the rabbits and birds. These things became a comfort to him. He grew to know a certain crow which, or so it appeared, suggested by a repeated caw-cawing and eager expression about the head, to both *recognise* Tubbs and to accept him in his territory (which encompassed Dodgson's view). Clumsy and shy, Radulph Tubbs was fingering the remote outskirts of sentiment. On clear days he forgot himself and for hours on end looked up at the sky. The sky, *sans* smokestacks, now held a certain delight. Its mutability brought to mind my sister's eyes, her magic; its mild expanse embraced him as nothing ever had before. He who had never considered his own infancy recalled how once as a tiny boy and looking up and giddy with a presentiment of infinity, he had fallen down.

One afternoon when Dodgson set off alone for the theatre, Radulph did not follow him but instead waited patiently for his return. The exercise of patience had become an end in itself. In his memoirs Radulph writes sincerely (if pedantically):

'Waiting I became aware of Time's inexorable process and my own finitude.'

More and more often Radulph forgot just *who* or *what* he was waiting for and so strolled aimlessly in any direction, the sport of every wind, his wet shoes sinking into the grass, his whiskers drooping, his arms akimbo, his eyes sad. For the very first time he received the world as a soft, impressionable clay. These days he rarely spoke, even to his servants; he thought that in the past he had spoken far too much. He was prey to melancholy: despite his vast wealth and the immoderate success of all his holdings, Radulph entertained the visceral conviction of inevitable ruin and incalculable loss.

But while this transformation was taking place, as Tubbs strolled and pondered and—when he remembered to—spied on Dodgson, he was himself the object of intense interest and ceaseless scrutiny: the *Hungerkünstler* was back from Egypt with a smuggler's fortune, her sails bloated with temper, her preposterous girth concealed in capes and carriages. If only Baconfield could have seen it! I believe he could have charted their orbits and the worst avoided. But Baconfield was in Bedlam, seized in the silent contemplation of Cobb.

The *Hungerkünstler* did not strike Radulph down at once. She was acutely perplexed by his transformation. Having abandoned his chimneys and suet puddings alike, the beefy, blustering bully she had known had metamorphosed into a wastrel perambulating in an indeterminate haze. And so the rage which had claimed her the day Radulph had abandoned her to the scorn and the scorpions of Sakkârah did not abate but instead hung suspended in a species of hot parentheses. And the little pearl-handled pistol she had brought with her from Cairo remained braced in a garter where it chafed her thigh.

Fingering that raw spot, the *Hungerkünstler* sat in her carriage and watched the man who had dumped her with a morbid curiosity and astonishment as well. It appeared that Radulph was dreaming; what could the insufferable braggart have to dream about?

As she contemplated Tubbs, who stood lax and unselfconscious among the trees, she gloated upon the amplitude of her intention: the amputation of a life. It made her feel immeasurably powerful, somehow divine.

How she hated him! She who hated the entire universe had made him its symbol. She recalled how the unwashed women in their tattered shrouds had come shrieking and hallooing from all directions, how they had led her, a piteous figure, parched nearly to death and absurdly dressed, to Baconfield's filthy hut; how Baconfield, once so dapper, had sat in the dust staring at the crusts on his feet—crowned fool in a kingdom of paupers, everything falling into decay about him, even the sky which was dropping its trashed stars.

The bells of Christ Church Chapel rang, and the *Hungerkünstler*, being a child of Hell, put her hands to her ears. As for Tubbs, startled from out his own revery, he trembled and a curious smile played about his lips. As the sound fined away he felt himself nucleate—just as upon the night of Zephyra's performance. Arrested and intent, he stood thrilled to the marrow: Etheria was there, pulsing and hovering within his breast, and all the newly disentombed cities of his mind were bathed in light.

Suddenly the *Hungerkünstler* knew: Radulph was dreaming about the wife who had run away! He was dreaming about Angus Sphery's daughter! He was dreaming about *Etheria!* The creature's jealous rage rose within her like a great, black wind. She cried out to her coachman to strike the horses without mercy, to batter them, to bring forth foam and blood. Screaming, the beasts pawed the air, then tore forward, thundering past Radulph and on and over his horizon. Seeing them he grieved but knew not why.

CHAPTER
23

O ur father, Angus Sphery, once described how certain butterflies risk their lives sailing the infinite airs above the seas to flock together at the *resonant place* (as he called it): an obscure tree, a ragged expanse of beach, a certain plain littered with glacial rubble—utterly transforming the landscape for a few, brief hours, before sailing off together to regions unknown, in one great, lucent cloud. This seemed a miracle to me, and if I recall it today, it is because one morning in November something similar took place in Baconfield's mind: he awoke to see spots, powdery, bright and ringed with black—like the eyes on the wings of butterflies. His mind was vagrant with moths, each with two pairs of eyes burning on the wings. And Baconfield could hear their small voices, the voices of angels, very high and thin, the sound the rim of a crystal champagne glass makes when rubbed with a wet finger.

Baconfield perceived that Cobb was far more agitated than usual. No longer did he appear to be rowing an invisible boat but instead struggled across a terrain of knee-high craters each lipped by a one-sided rim. Up, down and around, falling again and again, Cobb struggled across the vast, frigid room they shared as if attempting to escape something. Feeling anxious himself, Baconfield could not help but look furtively over his own shoulder and into the room's stubborn shadows bristling with dust.

By the sounds which reached them from other quarters, Baconfield knew that the entire asylum was in a frenzy. There was far more howling than customary and the air collapsed beneath the bludgeons of the guards and leapt to their whips. Baconfield, pinned to the same spots for months, stood up and on tender feet began to pace, taking care to circumvent the obstacles Cobb continued to maneuver so painfully. Through the rents in Cobb's trousers, Baconfield saw bruises. But when he attempted to keep Cobb from tumbling once again to the floor, he was savagely bitten. For the rest of the day, Baconfield sulked, nursing his arm and scowling.

Tubbs was strangely agitated too, although he was not aware of it. He was forever wandering in the wind, so taken with longing and remorse that he never noticed the great, fat woman who followed him everywhere, sitting in the back of a large, black hansom, breathing labouriously behind her veil.

What had happened to the man who had once been as square and solid as the Royal Bank of England? He had forgotten Dodgson entirely, he had forgotten his holdings, he no longer cared a fig for profits, social assemblies, Stilton. Indeed, so abstracted was he that all but his house-keeper had abandoned him, absconding with cutlery, fur coats, and small pieces of furniture. The house was stripped of andirons, counterpanes, and piss-pots. Had he wanted to, he couldn't have found a corkscrew.

His housekeeper, too old to consider going farther down the street than the chemist's, kept the fire going in his rooms and a joint in the oven, the rubbery slices of which Tubbs picked over listlessly, pushing them around and around in their cold mint jelly, when long after dinnertime he appeared, worn out and soaked to the skin. He was very thin now, his whiskers devoured his face, and his clothes drooped from his bony shoulders like diseased feathers. He had the lost, hurt look of an abandoned domestic animal; he looked homeless and haggard; he looked like someone who has never recovered from an emergency.

One bitter evening as Radulph was sitting alone in self-fumblement sucking a biscuit by the fire, Baconfield's nephew rang at the street door and was ushered in.

'Zephyra is back!' He said this dramatically, flourishing a large poster he had carried in tightly rolled and tucked beneath his arm. Then bending at the waist and peering into Radulph's face: 'Ye Gods!

You look like hell!' Tubbs stared at the poster stupidly. Misinterpreting his silence, Baconfield's nephew took a step backwards and apologised: 'I'm the fool—forgive me! Such painful memories! That madman Cobb! Your fractured jaw!'

Tubbs's face reddened. He began to glow. He was slapping his arms as if to spur on his circulation. He thought: *To see her!*

'You might wish to inform the agency?' queried Baconfield's nephew. 'The buggers might have informed *you*,' he added.

Tubbs's excitement was visibly rising. He paced the room leaving muddy tracks. He glowered at Baconfield's nephew. He wanted to *see* her. Not to *arrest* her. Not to harm her in any way... He would not even approach her! He had forfeited that right.

'Considering the rumpus you made the last time,' Baconfield's nephew mused, 'it is astonishing that she dares reappear, here in Oxford, and under the same name! It's been how long? Three years.'

Tubbs spoke at last: 'It *is* curious,' he murmured, quickening to an obscure thrill of hope. Perhaps, despite the risks, she wanted to see him again herself. She knew, had to know, that he had uncovered her alias. And yet she was back, in Oxford again, performing at the Metaphysic, just as before. She was orbiting Oxford, a luminous moon.

Tubbs took the poster from Baconfield's nephew and read it as best he could; the puissance of his emotion made it difficult for him to focus. This time she had been given star billing. Over the past few years she had toured the great capitals of the world: London, Paris, the Winter Gardens of Berlin, New York, Mexico City, Manaus—even Alexandria and Cairo. The world was at her feet!

Radulph was submerged in a tranquil tenderness unlike anything he had ever known, light years away from immoderate impulses. He thought that perhaps she had chosen to forgive him. This was her delicate way of saying: *I am here. If you choose to take me, I am yours.* This invitation emboldened him. Whatever had happened, as monstrous as he had been, *he had been her husband after all and she had done him an evil turn by vanishing.* But now she was back! What did it mean? What could it possibly mean? He said:

'What *can* it possibly mean?'

'The show is at nine.' Baconfield's nephew added, 'Dear fellow—

fumigate that vile tabernacle of yours! You smell like a buffalo!'

Tubbs stumbled off, his head swarming with memories. Well within the hour he returned, whiskers trimmed, and swimming in a fresh set of clothes.

'My teeth are loose,' he said.

'My snared partridge!' Baconfield's nephew sighed. 'What's to become of you?' And later, as they had settled themselves in the carriage, 'and can we be certain it *is* she?'

'It can only be Etheria,' Tubbs breathed.

'Yes . . . yes . . . but how do you know?'

'Because she has named her act *The Jade Cabinet!*' Baconfield's nephew was too perplexed to speak further, but his two cream-coloured horses, their harnesses stiff with cold and creaking in the wind, neighed in agreement.

Once when the carriage lurched, Radulph recalled with a devastating pang the time he had taken my sister against her will in a moving carriage. For the hundredth time he asked himself why he had imposed, and with such imperious callousness, what, under other circumstances, with other means, might have delighted her.

Strangely, as he looked out at the windswept streets glistening with a cold, persistent rain, he reeled with nostalgia for Egypt and this because there Etheria's memory had so haunted him that every minaret, date tree, dragoman, and donkey, the hovels of Fayûm and even the Zabtīyeh train station had each been perceived through the imperceptible mist which was his passion for my sister.

Suddenly, knowing he was at last on his way to see his lost love for her sake and not his own, he felt light, even giddy—like a man bringing a gift to his bride. The gift was selfhood, and Radulph wanted nothing in exchange. Although . . .

Once at the theatre he felt even jolly. *This is madness*, thought Baconfield's nephew; *the old man deludes himself. It is unreasonable that he should be happy!* He felt sorry for his friend whom, it seemed, had shrunken in size; as he put his arm around Radulph's shoulder he was shocked to feel how fragile he had become.

They entered the theatre just as the curtain was rising; two seats remained down near the front, not far from the orchestra pit.

The snake charmer, a pale, lithesome lad of little more than twenty and unusually tall, appeared first. He undulated about the stage with an anaconda as thick as himself. The beast's milky mouth, bristling with needlelike teeth, could have easily severed the boy's head from his neck with one bite.

The boy orbited the stage in a narrowing circle until he stood perfectly immobile, ringed from head to foot in scales. The snake's head came to rest upon his shoulder and from there peered out at the audience apparently with greed. There they stood as fixed as a symbol for sexual determinism, or an emblem of mortal combat. Tubbs found that he was gasping for air, seized with excitement and thrust into moral disorder. As the curtain fell he began to dream, imagining that after the performance he and Baconfield's nephew would step out into the street and Etheria would suddenly burst from a stage door in the alley, a robe hastily thrown over her shoulders, and calling out to him, fall upon her knees imploring his forgiveness, Baconfield's nephew sighing as he eclipsed: 'Lucky man!' But even if she saw him from the stage, would she recognise him? He was so very grey now and thin and worn. He looked down at his own bony hands in disgust. He was a husk. The kernel gnawed out. He was old.

But now the curtain was once more rising upon a stage flooded with blue light, and Radulph trembled with terror and delight, reduced to his heart's essential honey. That mysterious bell sounded, the smell of roses filled the air, and she appeared surrounded by slender boys manipulating screens and cabinets and ladders.

This time her act was based upon a series of disappearances, each one acutely painful to Tubbs. Zephyra vanished from within coffins, metal cages, cabinets perched on top of pedestals; from ladders and plates of glass; from within aquariums and lacquer chests, from behind flags: the whole evolved so swiftly, with such subtlety and splendour, that her audience was dazzled. If before she had been wonderful, this time she was a breathing wind, the six wings of Daniel's angels! I know, because I too was there.

When Zephyra began her most celebrated act, juggling with those familiar spheres of glass as she appeared to stand suspended on the air,

Radulph, nearly delirious, and fearing that she would suddenly vanish again and forever, rose from his chair and raised his arms as if to implore her to descend from the ether and to stand upon the stage; above all to stay, not to move from that spot but to stand there forever in the blue light, the eternal captive of his eyes.

Just then a shadow appeared. It loomed up from the front row, but a few yards from the stage. With horror, Radulph recognized the *Hungerkünstler*. She stared at him with loathing and perhaps disdain before, seeming to smile, she turned away. He saw her broad back and the veil that rose from her shoulders like a black wing, and it was then, as he thought *like a black wing*, that a shot exploded in the air and Zephyra's strangely beautiful face was blown apart. The many spheres of glass tumbled to the floor and shattered; a few rolled off into the shadows with a clatter. Her body fell after, as if it were lighter. She lay immobile in a debris of fractured mirrors and splintered wood, splattered with blood and horribly disfigured.

Radulph stood as if petrified; now everyone was standing. He heard screams and sobbing; he did not realise that he was himself screaming, the low, guttural sound a man makes when he hangs. There was a commotion in the front row; the *Hungerkünstler* was heaving herself across his horizon and she was retching. She was arrested in the street.

CHAPTER
24

It was I who bathed Zephyra's fractured face; I who wiped the clotted blood from her hair and who laid her out in her very best—I found in her battered clothes-trunk a pale blue sequined dress, a pair of silver shoes, kid gloves. . . When I said *I am her sister*, no one disbelieved me; I believed it myself. It was not until I had undressed her, had removed the bloody garments from her perfect corpse, that I was faced with the truth: Zephyra was not my sister; Zephyra was a man. I, who had never seen a naked man before, looked upon his body with bittersweet regret and such a rush of sensuality that under other circumstances I should have at once chastised myself. Why did I appropriate her subterfuge? Even now I cannot say.

I dressed her, I implored the doctor to leave the poor body in peace. He stuck a finger in the wound, looked into the corpse's eyes and left. The police asked only that I sign some documents. I brought in the priest and without ceremony had the body buried in the family plot. (For a time I feared someone might claim her; no one did.) And then I waited for Radulph to come. It took him time—he had been so badly shaken—but he came at last with roses for the grave, and flowers for myself as well—his first gift to me. We set off for the cemetery and I saw that he was much diminished; I was sensitive to the great many changes that had taken place in his heart.

At the end of our hour together, he asked if he could see me again. He told me that he wished to show me certain things that he had written down, memories and idle thoughts; he hoped these might explain him-self to me, that if I read all that he had written, I might be willing to forgive him, at least enough to be, from time to time, accepted into my circle. I told him I had no circle. This appeared to startle him and he took my hand. I felt an intense surprise as no man had ever taken my hand before. I thought: *Foolish child! He is old enough to be your grandfather!*

A few weeks later Radulph appeared at my door with more flowers—orchids, a flamboyant choice—the Spanish nougat I have never ceased to love, and a thick book filled with his deeply slanted scrawl.

'These are my scribbles,' he said, 'insensate atoms.' He coughed, suddenly embarrassed. 'The only way I can bring my volatile thoughts together . . .' I was amazed when he continued: 'Being here tonight with you is . . .'

We were in the drawing room which I knew must have been pain-fully familiar although my father's shelves were barren of books, eggs, butterflies.

'I thought,' said he, 'that your order-loving and gentle eye might find some sense or truth in all this and even, perhaps, the manifold potentialities of my own soul.'

Our life together was in all ways uneventful if pleasant enough, although I was oft plagued by the thought that my sister Etheria might reappear just as suddenly as she had vanished. Yet I doubted, having never wanted him, that she would have asked for Radulph back. And I knew that a magician of extraordinary capacities was touring the American conti-nent. Her name: Carmen Khamsin.

Deep down I knew I should never again see Etheria, for if, as our father Angus Sphery believed, there exists a Divine Tongue capable of bringing all things into being, *the opposite is also true.* Etheria had found the Word, surely a silent one, that had caused her to vanish forever from the life of Radulph Tubbs.

If I am now once again alone, still I appreciate having had a husband who in the eyes of the world was no bigamist but a widower and—of this I am certain—in the eyes of the Lord a reformed sinner. If the mills continued to bring in profits, these went (and still do) to charity.

Radulph lived simply in my father's house for five peaceful years, at the end of which he died. He lies beside the body of that unknown Adonis, Zephyra, as, to my dismay (no matter), he had specifically requested in his testament. I worry that when I too reach Heaven, Radulph and God alike will surely chastise me the lie.

AfterworD
WAKING TO EDEN

I was infected with the venom of language in early childhood when, sitting in a room flooded with sunlight, I opened an alphabet book. B was a Brobdingnagian tiger-striped bumblebee, hovering over a crimson blossom, its stinger distinct. This image was of such potency that my entire face—eyes, nose and lips—was seized by a phantom stinging, and my ears by a hallucinatory buzzing. In this way, and in an instant, I was simultaneously initiated into the alphabet and awakened to Eden.

In Eden, to see a thing Yahweh had dreamed and to say its name aloud was to bring it surging into the real. The letter B, so solid and threatening, *was* the bee; it was the embodiment of all its potencies. Looking at that letter, that blossom and that bee was like looking into a mirror from which the skin had been peeled away. The page afforded a passage—transcendental and yet altogether tangible.

Much later I learned that for the Kabbalist, Beth is female and passive—a little house waiting to be prodded by the thrusting dart of letter A. Aleph, knowing that Beth will always be there, her door open in expectancy, boldly confronts the universe: O vigorous, confident, *thrusting* Aleph! (Now I know, too, just how *erotic* the image was—those engorged petals about to be ravished! Perhaps my sensuous life is here somehow reduced to its essential honey!)

Just as once Persian wizards read a sacred text on the bodies of tigers, I had, from that morning, entered into an exulted state from which I was never to entirely recover, expecting, no, *demanding* enchantment each time I opened a book. That letter **B** convinced me of what I think I already knew—that the world is a ceremonial dialogue to be actively engaged, and life's intention the searching out of the fertile passages and places, a fearless looking for the thorny **A** and **B** in everything.

A wood stretched behind the house; it was a place of wild hives, seed rattles, lost feathers, quartz fragments (and occasional arrowheads), and the gods themselves materializing in variable forms: horned beetle, red deer, fox, owl, snake (this was copperhead country), death-head moth, hawk, hummingbird; stinkweed also, and a treacherous mud with a will of its own whose depth, in certain seasons, could not be determined. So many of the games I played there read now like rites of passage. I was very aware of danger—supernatural and actual; every time I penetrated into the wood I crossed a threshold from one cosmic dimension into another.

Each element of the wood implied a magical possibility; each element was, in fact, a potent letter, and all was contained—or so it seemed—in one vast *magic act*. I could not see a lady bug without entering into the ritual:

> *Lady bug, lady bug, fly away home!*
> *Your house is on fire! Your children have gone!*

It was here that I confronted death for the first time—in the shape of a fox, its inert body animated by a swarm of bees. I stood transfixed beside that vortex and knew *transformation* defines and rules the world. And because I had, in a room which now seemed worlds away, been myself changed forever by a letter in a book, I crouched and left a votive gift sublimely *transitional*, before moving on deeper into the world's wood—those gorgeous and terrifying images—like a necromantic alphabet of molten glass—pulsing behind my eyes.

I like to imagine that Adam's tongue, his palate and his lips were always on fire, that the air he breathed was kindled to incandescence each time he cried out in sorrow or delight. If fiction can be said to have a function, it is to release that primary fury of which language, even now, is miraculously capable—from the dry mud of daily use. So that furred, spotted and striped, it may—as it did in Eden—scrawl under every tree as revelation.

Language is magic—transforming dead snakes into animate nature. When language fails, as when memory fails, all we can hope for is an airless cabinet reeking of badly preserved specimens!

In *The Jade Cabinet*, Etheria metamorphoses from victim—a creature in a jar—to magician, an animating air, a vital breath. The 'Book of Air,' *The Jade Cabinet* is the fourth and final novel in a 'Tetralogy of Elements': Radulph Tubbs, so weighty, is, when he rises, inflated by vanity, and the *Hungerkünstler*, who at the start lives on air, evolves into a murderously bad wind. Like the other books in the tetralogy, *The Jade Cabinet* investigates the processes of fabulating, creating and remembering.

In *The Fountains of Neptune* (Water), the magician is language, and memory the key to infancy, selfhood and the soul's treasure house of dreams. Water is conjured as unstable weather; furiously boiling one moment, ice the next, it takes on the shapes of pools, whirlpools, downpours, oceans and tears. Dreams are *floating islands* (also the name of a dessert made with eggs; the philosophical egg appears throughout the tetralogy in variable guises) which—as all the food in *Neptune* (imagine trying to cook without water!)—induces forgetfulness.

Entering Fire, part poetry, part linguistic clamor, was intended to be read quickly—as one runs barefoot over embers. Its fires are sexual, intellectual and political, and its tensions Manichean. The cosmic battleground in *The Stain* (Earth) is the soul of a child disfigured by a birthmark in the shape of a dancing hare. Reduced to one potent sign, Charlotte eats glass and—just as Etheria—is rendered speechless.

All four novels investigate the end of Eden and the possibility of its reconstitution. I see them as Books of Nature and, because they are descriptive and painterly, as *Vanitas* and *Archetypa*, too. (I suppose, also, that because they all brood over singularities—ogresses, hunger artists, murderers and sirens—they could be said to fit into prodigy literature.)

My childhood heroes were Leeuwenhoek and Lewis Carroll; my ambition, never realized, to paint the museum scenery behind walruses and saber-toothed tigers. Even now I long for my own poetic territory which would include a keeping garden for insects, an extensive zoological library (color plates intact!), a wonder room and a jade cabinet which would, ideally, contain a chimera of mutton-fat jade.

—RIKKI DUCORNET

RIKKI DUCORNET is a transdisciplinary artist. Her work is animated by an interest in nature, Eros, tyranny, and the transcendent capacities of the creative imagination. She is a poet, fiction writer, essayist, and artist, and her fiction has been translated into fifteen languages. Her art has been exhibited internationally, most recently with Amnesty International's traveling exhibit I Welcome, focused on the refugee crisis. She has received numerous fellowships and awards including an Arts and Letters Award from the American Academy of Arts and Letters, the Charles Flint Kellogg Award in Arts and Letters from Bard College, the Prix Guerlain, and the Lannan Literary Award for Fiction. Her novel *The Jade Cabinet* was a finalist for the National Book Critics Circle Award. She lives in Port Townsend, Washington.

Printed in the USA
CPSIA information can be obtained
at www.ICGtesting.com
JSHW020011140824
68050JS00002B/3